"Dinky Hocker has a mother so dedicated to her precious dope addicts that she has no sympathy for persons with other problems. Not for her daughter, Dinky, who has this terrific fat problem. Not for Dinky's cousin Natalia, who rhymes when she gets nervous and has to go to a special school for the mentally disturbed. Not for Tucker, who has never had a meaningful relationship in his life. And certainly not for P. John, whose father is so liberal that P. John has turned into a 15-year-old middle-aged square in self-defense. . . . The most difficult problems are Dinky's—whose addiction to food makes her life a nightmare . . . until the night of her shocking explosion, when at last some people understand you don't have to be a public loser to have private troubles."—*The New York Times*

M. E. Kerr was born in Auburn, New York, and attended the University of Missouri. Until recently, she lived in Brooklyn Heights, the setting of her book, but now lives in Long Island, New York.

ALSO AVAILABLE IN LAUREL-LEAF BOOKS:

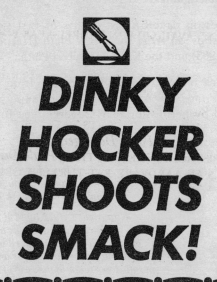

DINKY HOCKER SHOOTS SMACK!

A NOVEL BY

M. E. Kerr

Acknowledgements

the lines on page 57, last 4 lines of first stanza of "Lesbos" in *Ariel* by Sylvia Plath (Harper & Row, 1965) and the Estate of Sylvia Plath.

the lines on pages 12, 14, and 111 from *The Little Prince* by Antoine de Saint-Exupéry reprinted by permission of Harcourt Brace Jovanovich.

Published by
Dell Publishing Co., Inc.
1 Dag Hammarskjold Plaza
New York, New York 10017

ISBN: 0-440-92030-2

RL: 5.7

Printed in the United States of America
September 1973
20

WFH

ONE

"DON'T TELL people we've moved to Brooklyn," Tucker Woolf's father always told him. "Tell them we've moved to Brooklyn *Heights*."

"Why? Brooklyn Heights is Brooklyn."

"Believe me, Tucker, you'll make a better impression."

Which was very important to Tucker's father—making a good impression. That fact was one of the reasons Tucker felt sorry for his father now. It was hard to make a good impression when you'd just been fired.

No sooner had they moved from Gramercy Park in Manhattan to Joralemon Street in Brooklyn Heights, then Tucker's father lost his job. At the same time, he developed an allergy to cats. That meant Tucker had to give away Nader.

Nader was a nine-month-old calico cat Tucker had found under a Chevrolet the first night they moved into their new Heights town house. Tucker had named the cat Ralph Nader, who had done his own time under Chevrolets. But when Tucker discovered he was a she, he had shortened her name to Nader.

Nader had lived for three months with the Woolfs, until Tucker's father began wheezing and sneezing at the sight of her.

In Brooklyn Heights when you wanted to find something or get rid of something, you put a sign up on a tree.

Tucker's sign read:

DO YOU FEEL UNWANTED, IN THE WAY, AND THE CAUSE OF EVERYONE'S MISERY? ARE YOU TALKED ABOUT BEHIND YOUR BACK AND PLOTTED AGAINST? THEN YOU KNOW HOW I FEEL. I AM A CALICO KITTEN PUTTING MYSELF UP FOR ADOPTION. I HAVE ALREADY BEEN SPAYED BY DR. WASSERMAN OF HICKS STREET, AND I AM IN GOOD CONDITION PHYSICALLY. MENTALLY I AM ON A DOWNER, THOUGH, UNTIL I RELOCATE. IF YOU KNOW HOW A LOSER FEELS AND WANT TO HELP, CALL MAIN 4-8415.

The only one who called was Dinky Hocker of Remsen Street. She came waddling down to Joralemon and took Nader away in a plaid carrying case, telling Tucker to visit the cat whenever he felt like it.

At first Tucker went there often. But after a while he stopped going, because of what was happening to Nadar. Dinky, who was fourteen, a year younger than Tucker, ate all the time. She fed Nader all the time, too. Dinky was five foot four and weighed around 165. Now Nader was toddling around like something that had had too much air pumped into it. Her eyes were glazed over with too many memories of too much mackerel, steak, raw egg, hamburger, milk, and tuna fish.

Nadar knew how to retrieve empty, wadded-up cigarette packages. But on Tucker's last visit to her, she had refused even to get up on her feet at the sound of the cellophane crinkling. She had cocked one eye, looked at Tucker forlornly, and sank back into a calorie-drugged sleep.

Although Tucker stopped visiting Nader, he didn't stop thinking about her. He had never owned a pet, and to have found this one huddled under a car, flea-ridden and runny-eyed, made him feel all the more responsible toward her.

"Somehow," Tucker's mother had commented, "you identify with that cat, and I don't see why. You've never been a stray. You've always been loved. Is there anything you've ever really wanted that you couldn't have?"

"I guess not."

"Then why all the concern over this animal? She has a perfectly good home now."

"I just don't think a cat should weigh about two tons, that's all!"

"Hey, Tucker," his father said. "What did the

two-ton canary say as he prowled down the dark alley late at night?"

"I don't know," Tucker said. "What *did* the two-ton canary say?" But he knew. It was such an old joke.

Tucker's father said, "Here Kitty, Kitty. Here Kitty, Kitty."

Tucker's mother laughed unusually hard at the joke. She had been overdoing everything where Tucker's father was concerned, ever since he'd lost his job. She pretended it took great effort to stop laughing. Then she told Tucker. "You're probably right to just put that cat out of your mind. Don't go over to the Hockers' anymore. I thought Dinky would be a nice new friend for you, but don't go if it gets you worrying about the cat!"

Tucker attended private school in Manhattan. Afternoons, when he got back to Brooklyn, he often went directly to the Heights branch of the Brooklyn Public Library. It was easier to study there. Tucker's father and uncle spent their afternoons at the town house dreaming up some new scheme that was supposed to make them both millionaires in five years. They hadn't said yet what the scheme was. Their discussions were noisy and argumentative. Around four thirty, they always began "the official cocktail hour," which made them noisier and lasted until Tucker's mother returned from her temporary job.

Tucker was an authority on libraries. He went to them as often as drunks did to dry out and read up on their symptoms in the medical books; and as often as crazies did to talk to themselves in corners and warm themselves by radiators.

As a small boy, Tucker had been allowed to watch only fourteen hours of television a week. He could watch whatever he chose to watch, and if he wanted to spend one day watching television for fourteen hours straight, he could do that. But he could never watch more than fourteen hours a week.

He had become a reader and a sketcher. In the libraries of New York he found he could do both easier than anywhere else.

As a reader, he was what his mother called a "dilettante." A dabbler. He often didn't finish books and magazines he started. If he checked six books out of the library to take home to read, he never got around to reading any of them. It was the way his father was about their eating in neighborhood restaurants. They never ate in them. His father always said, "We'll get around to them eventually. Let's try something not so close at hand."

But *in* the library, Tucker could read parts of as many books as he wanted to. It was a smorgasbord.

As an artist, Tucker was what his mother called "a depressing Bosch." The first time she had called him that, he had asked why. She had answered, "Bosch, as in Hieronymus Bosch. Look it up." His mother was a great researcher on every subject, but she never did anyone else's research for him.

This was what Tucker found under Bosch, Hieronymus:

> *A Dutch painter known for his scenes of
> nightmarish tortures in hell at the hands of
> weird monsters.*

Tucker had looked up the paintings of Bosch.
With his mother's special talent for overstate-
ment, he could see why she would say that. Tucker's scenes of library life were odd imaginings:
the prissy-looking, middle-aged woman with seams
in her stockings, checking out a book with
"corpse" in the title, should be sketched with a
limp hand hanging out of her purse. In a balloon
above her head would be a line of handless people
marching into a hand laundry. The nervous-look-
ing man back by the law books, reading up on
leases with his overcoat on and necktie loosened,
would be sketched reading in a chair before an
apartment house, with all his furniture piled
around him on the sidewalk, in a snowstorm.

As a sketcher, Tucker could find a face smorgasbord in the libraries, too. It seemed too him sometimes that anyone with any trouble at all eventually found his way to a city library, and the really
troubled ones became regulars. Their features
were wrecked with disappointment and forebear-
ance. Tucker would look for them at the Epiphany
branch on East 23rd, back near the religious books;
in the basement reference room at the Jefferson in
Greenwich Village; in the lobby at Donnell in the

West Fifties; the whole of Tompkins Square, and Circulating in the 42nd Street main branch. Tucker loved wrecked faces, sad smiles, and soft tones, and the libraries of New York abounded in them.

But of all the libraries Tucker had ever visited, the one in Brooklyn Heights was hands down the winner.

Tucker had intended to write a long poem about it and how it wasn't phony like many. It didn't pull something like putting books almost as old as *My Antonia* in the Pay Duplicate section and charging you five cents a day to read it. It had no Pay Duplicate section, in fact. It was air-conditioned. It had bathrooms and telephone booths and lockers. It was like what someone had once said about the difference between being rich and poor: rich was better. It was plush.

One afternoon, a week before Thanksgiving, Tucker had gone there to work on a poem for his Creative Writing class. The poem was supposed to have a theme of "thanks for something out-of-the-ordinary."

Tucker's poem was about the library. For that reason he would never finish it or show it to anyone. He was aware that a male cat-lover, who was also a lover of libraries, was better off keeping all that to himself. Another fact he kept to himself was his ambition to be a librarian. He figured he'd announce it one day in college, after he'd scored the winning touchdown in a football game or won high honors in some course like Outer Space Cartography.

His poem began:

> *I never thought that anything I'd like best,*
> *Would be located on Cadman Plaza West,*
> *In Brooklyn.*

He jotted it down on the outside of his spiral notebook, saw its promise, abandoned it, and put on his coat. It was five o'clock. In the days when he was still visiting Nader, it was the time he'd start over to Remsen Street.

Instead, he headed down Clinton and turned into Pierrepont, and because Brooklyn Heights was the way he'd heard the English were about animals, he saw cats on stoops, with bells and nametags around their necks, saucers left on windowsills for cats, cats looking down from windows, and cats sunning themselves under lamps in people's parlors. There were dogs everywhere, too, but Tucker had become a cat man.

Tucker had to pass the First Unitarian Church. On the lawn in front was a sermon board behind glass. Instead of the Sunday sermon title and the names of the ministers, there was always a saying on the board: a line from a poem or book.

That afternoon there was something taken from *The Little Prince* by Antoine de Saint-Exupéry.

> *If you tame me, then we shall need each other.*
> *To me, you will be unique in all the world. To*
> *you, I shall be unique in all the world.*

Tucker got a sudden flash of Nader sitting under the Chevrolet on Henry Street the evening he found her. He could remember taking her home under his jacket and telling her not to be wild, everything was going to be okay for her. In fact, he told her, she had walked into a very good deal. That was the truth, too, because Tucker's father hadn't been fired yet. He hadn't been allergic yet. He'd simply been this professional fund raiser Tucker'd always known him to be. No sweat about money problems. No postnasal drip. He hadn't even minded Nader's litter pan in the bathroom.

Tucker got another flash, not of the past, but of the future: Nader keeling over one day, finished from a massive coronary at nine months. Dr. Wasserman, the Heights vet, told the assembled mourners, "This kitten was stuffed to death." That was what Tucker's father had once said about a client: "His wife stuffed him to death until he suffered a massive coronary."

Tucker's mother had corrected the statement. "His wife stuffed him until he had a massive coronary and died," she said. "He didn't have the massive coronary after he died, dear."

Tucker's mother had her PhD in English Lit. She had once been an editor. Now she was working as one again, temporarily. Just as Tucker was not supposed to say they had moved to Brooklyn, and was supposed to say Brooklyn *Heights,* so was Tucker not supposed to say his mother worked on

Stirring Romances, and was supposed to say she worked for Arrow Publications.

If you tame me, then we shall need each other.

Tucker Woolf was tall for his age, with a certain way of standing which had landed him in Corrective Posture two years in a row. He was blue-eyed and bespectacled, with chin-length straight black hair. He shifted his book bag from his right hand to his left. He straightened his shoulders and stopped looking down at the street. It was time to take a stand.

If it would make his father feel better, he was willing to remember to add Heights to Brooklyn when he said where he lived. If it would make his father feel better, he was willing to say his mother's temporary job was at Arrow Publications, never mentioning the crummy magazine which employed her. He was willing, in life, to be discreet, diplomatic, subtle, gentle and forgiving; but there were times when this behavior was wrong.

Tucker Woolf marched across Pierrepont past the Appellate Division of the State Supreme Court, down Henry Street past the Church of Our Lady of Lebanon, and across and down Remsen Street almost to the river. He thought of how he had forced himself to concentrate in Dinky Hocker's presence, so he would never even say something accidental like "fat chance" or "fathead" or "the fat's in the fire." He had handled the whole enormous problem with kid gloves and kindness; but there were times when this behavior was wrong.

He stopped before a red brownstone with a yellow door, went up the stone steps, and lifted the brass knocker.

Dinky herself answered.

Dinky had dusty blond hair, and her cheeks flushed from the slighest exertion. She favored ersatz articles of clothing, like her father's tweed-suit vest worn over a T-shirt, with green cotton pajama bottoms and old white tennis socks.

That was the way she was dressed as she answered the door.

"I thought you weren't going to exercise your visiting rights anymore," she said. Dinky's father was a lawyer, and her conversation was sometimes peppered with legal jargon.

"I just dropped by to tell you I doubt that Nader's happy having a weight problem," Tucker said. "I doubt that you are, either. But you've given her your problem and it isn't fair."

"She's given me a problem, too," Dinky said, undaunted by this sudden pronouncement. "She's scratched her claws on our Hide-A-Bed and ruined it, just when we need it."

"You didn't even listen," Tucker said, walking into the foyer and setting down his book bag. "I'm going to stay until it sinks in, Dinky! Nader doesn't deserve your problems."

"*No one* deserves my problems," Dinky said.

"Why do you have to feed her so much?"

"Don't worry," Dinky said. "We've got another mouth to feed, suddenly. We'll be lucky if there's enough to go around."

"What are you talking about?"

"I'm talking about my cousin."

Then suddenly from behind Dinky this girl appeared.

The first thing Tucker noticed was her eyes. They were very bright, and Tucker found himself wanting to smile at the girl, as though they both had some sort of mischief as a secret between them, maybe on Dinky, maybe not. But there was a definite vibration, an exchange, and Tucker almost did smile, except Tucker rarely smiled. He smiled to himself, usually; no one could tell. But he had an idea this girl could tell. Her own smile grew all the broader.

"This is the other mouth," Dinky said, her hand sweeping grandly and cynically toward the girl. There was something old-fashioned-looking about the girl. She was wearing a navy-blue jumper and a white blouse with long, billowing sleeves. She was wearing a string of pearls, white stockings, and black shoes. The girl was how old? Older than Tucker? Younger? The same age? He wasn't sure. Her hair was black and it spilled down past her shoulders. Her eyes were green like Nader's, and her skin was very smooth and very white.

"I'm Tucker Woolf," Tucker said, because Dinky forgot to introduce them beyond announcing that the girl was the other mouth.

"I'm Natalia Line."

"Fine," Tucker said, embarrassed because it rhymed.

"Natalia has a fine line," the girl laughed. "Natalia has a fine, divine line," she continued, laughing all the harder, "a fine divine line, that's mine," and her eyes were flashing.

Tucker didn't laugh easily. He didn't like silly girls. He wouldn't have liked the whole scene at any other time, but somehow it was different because of this girl. He smiled at her. Then he laughed out loud.

Tucker's mother often used to say whenever he laughed, "Oh, don't tell me you're going to choke up some youthful laughter, Tucker!" because he was usually so solemn.

Dinky Hocker was the only one who wasn't amused. "We have a walking, talking, rhyming dictionary living with us," she said very sarcastically, "and I can tell you I'm thrilled about *that*."

TWO

IT WAS late in the morning, the day after Thanksgiving.

"Four times this week." Tucker woke up to hear his mother's voice coming from the kitchen, where she was breakfasting with his father. He remembered that his mother had the day off, too.

"To see the cat?" his father's voice asked.

"No."

"Oh?"

"This niece of Helen Hocker is staying with them now."

"He goes to see her?"

"Yes. With the excuse he's visiting the cat."

"Ah!"

"Cal, I think he's—"

"In love?"

"Yes."

"No."

"Why not? He's fifteen."

"Just barely."

"Nevertheless."

Tucker sat up in bed and shouted, "Now that you've got that all settled, can I have some breakfast?"

"*May* I have some breakfast," his mother called back, "and it isn't polite to eavesdrop, Tucker."

"Then try to remember I sleep practically in the kitchen," said Tucker.

"That was your idea, Mister," his father answered. "Give me that room for a study, and you can have my study upstairs for a bedroom."

"Never mind," Tucker said. He was in his robe, making his way down the hall toward them.

His mother was still sitting at the kitchen table.

"May I have some breakfast?" Tucker asked. "Please."

"Yes, you may, dear." She got up and went across to the stove and Tucker's father poured himself more coffee and said, "There's an old Chinese saying: Man is what man hears he is, at keyhole."

"What you hear is what you get," said Tucker pulling out a chair.

"That expression's practically an anachronism now," his mother said.

His mother prided herself on being up on everything, including the youth scene. Last month for *Stirring Romances* she had helped write a confession story called "I Lost My Son At A Pot Party."

It wasn't what it sounded like; confession stories never were. It was about a woman whose little boy had wandered away from a party where a demonstrator was showing housewives how to cook with new nonstick pots. The title was supposed to pull in younger readers.

"Anyway, I'm not in love," Tucker said.

"Good. Then you'll be able to eat," his mother said. "I'm fixing you three eggs and some sausage."

"When I was fourteen," his father said, "I was in love with a girl named Marcia Spriggs. Our song was something about stars on high, winking why."

"It sounds really moving," Tucker said.

"In those days you could still make out the words to songs," his father said.

"Some words," Tucker answered. "Really passionate."

"No, you're not in love," Tucker's mother said. "Love makes you sweeter, and you sound pretty sour to me this morning."

" 'Stars on high, winking why,' " Tucker's father sang, " 'in the sky, why O why.' "

"What does Natalia Line look like?" Tucker's mother said, cracking eggs into the frying pan.

"That's hard to say," Tucker said. "There's something old-fashioned about her."

Tucker's father sang, " 'I saw an old-fashioned moon'—Hey, that song was popular circa Marcia Spriggs, too. 'I saw an old-fashioned moon; I heard an old-fashioned tune,' " he sang.

So much for communication, with Tucker's fa-

ther in a mood to make an old song out of anything anyone said.

Tucker finished his breakfast while his mother
and father swapped hit songs from the dark ages.
Then he dressed, changing his clothes three times
until he decided on jeans and a blue workman's
shirt, and his eight-inch lineman's boots with the
bright yellow laces.

After that he called the Hockers and learned
that Natalia was still wherever she'd gone for
Thanksgiving, and Dinky was down at Woerner's
Restaurant, picking up pies for Mrs. Hocker's Encounter Group that evening.

Mrs. Hocker was a do-gooder. She was lately
concentrating on young people who used to be
dope addicts.

She once told Tucker, "In a way, my young
people are all strays, just like your Nader was, only they aren't cute and cuddly like Nader, and no
one wants to take them in."

"On the other hand," Dinky had butted in,
"Nader wouldn't punch you in the face and grab
your purse, either."

"Neither would any of them anymore," Mrs.
Hocker had retaliated, "and you should be a little
kinder toward people who don't have the chance
in life you have."

Tucker put on his wool-plaid-lined blue-denim
utility jacket and prepared to head down toward
Woerner's, in search of Dinky.

"Don't forget to be back by five o'clock," his mother said. "At five o'clock your father and your uncle are going to unfold their new business scheme."

Tucker should have known that Dinky would still be at Woerner's, eating. To ask someone like Dinky to go into Woerner's Restaurant just to pick up pies for her mother was to ask a wino to drop in at a vineyard just to watch the bottling process.

Woerner's had the best food in Brooklyn Heights. All the lawyers from the courthouse and the Supreme Court building ate there at noon, and the restaurant had little sections called things like "The Caucus Room" to make the lawyers feel right at home. The talk in Woerner's was all about writs and judges and defenses and adjournments, while the lawyers wolfed down big plates of beef stroganoff, goulash with noodles, Königsberger klops, and sauerbraten.

Dinky was sitting at the counter finishing a plate of hot roast beef with home fries and fresh peas. She acknowledged Tucker's presence with little more than a raised eyebrow, and went right on eating and reading a book. Tucker waited five minutes for a place beside her at the counter. He ordered a piece of chocolate pie with whipped cream when he sat down, and Dinky told Agnes, the waitress, "Make that two, with a side of chocolate ice cream on mine."

Then she said to Tucker, "What are you doing

here? If you're looking for Natalia Rhyme, she's still away for the holidays."

"Where does she go for the holidays?" Tucker asked.

Dinky shrugged. "Who cares?"

Tucker didn't want to say that he cared, because Dinky was an unpredictable scenemaker. If Tucker had said, "Well, I care," Dinky would be just as liable to yell out, "OH, I SUPPOSE NOW YOU'RE IN LOVE WITH NATALIA LINE," and Tucker had had his fill of that kind of talk already.

Tucker decided to just hang around Dinky for a while and hope she would drop something into the conversation about when Natalia was returning. Or where Natalia had come from . . . or how long Natalia was going to stay with the Hockers . . . or anything about her, because Tucker really knew nothing about her.

"What are you reading?" he said.

"A book for a book report," she told him. "It's a book about John Merrick. I bet you've never even heard of him."

"I haven't."

"I knew it," she said. "No one's heard about him. He was grotesque. Whenever he went out he had to wear a black cloak and a cap the size of a basket, with a curtain falling to his shoulders, showing nothing but eyeholes."

"You're right. I never heard of him," Tucker said.

"He lived in Victorian England," Dinky said. "He had so much bone on his face and head that it pulled his mouth out of line and he couldn't make human sounds. He only had one eye, and his whole head was covered with these big cauliflower sacs which gave off a really putrid odor, and he didn't have hands."

"How can you read that and eat?" Tucker said.

"They wouldn't even take him in the circus," Dinky said. "He had to go everywhere in a carriage with drawn blinds."

She slammed the book shut. It was called *The Elephant Man: A Study In Human Dignity* by Ashley Montagu.

"I'm going to the library after this to find out more about him," Dinky said, as the waitress served them their pie. "He wasn't even bitter about it."

"He was probably psycho," Tucker said.

"Psychos aren't happy," Dinky said. "This guy was happy. He once said, 'I am happy every hour of the day.'"

"Then he had to be psycho," Tucker said. "No one's that happy."

"What you know about psychos would fill an ant's mouth," Dinky said, and then she began yelling at Agnes, the waitress, because she had forgotten to put the chocolate ice cream on the pie.

Earlier in the week, when Tucker had been over at the Hockers', Natalia had pinched his elbow to get his attention, and whispered, "Want to know a secret?" The three of them were sitting in Dinky's room watching color T.V., and Dinky was petting Nader and talking to her about Tucker and Natalia.

She was saying things like, "Well, Nader, Tucker says he's here to see you, but I don't think he's here to see you at all, do you think he's here to see you, Nader?" and things like, "I'll tell you something, Nader. When Tucker leaves, it seems Natalia doesn't have much to say to us. I guess we bore Natalia, Nader. Dinky Dull and Nader Nowhere—that's us, all right."

Tucker leaned toward Natalia to hear the secret.

"There's nothing wrong with Dinky's glands," Natalia said. "She's fat because every afternoon she goes to every restaurant in the Heights and eats something in each one. No one ever sees all she eats, because she never eats *all* she eats in one place."

"She's not supposed to eat out," Tucker said. He had heard Dinky's mother say that often enough.

"She does all her eating out," Natalia said. "She's sly. I like that."

Natalia was always surprising Tucker with tag endings like that. He'd go along thinking Natalia was just gossiping like any other catty female, and then it would turn out that she was secretly admiring the very behavior Tucker thought she was criticizing.

Once when she was telling Tucker about this boy in Mrs. Hocker's Friday night Encounter Group, she said, "And do you know what Mrs. Hocker found out about him? He's a recidivist."

25

"What's that?" Tucker had asked.

"That's someone who's gone back to an old habit. This boy had promised Mrs. Hocker and the group that he'd swear off pills. He was taking uppers before he joined the group. And Mrs. Hocker found out he started taking them again. He's a recidivist."

"Too bad," Tucker had commented.

"Why?" Natalia had said. "He needs those uppers. If Mrs. Hocker had been doing him any good, he wouldn't have gone back to taking uppers, would he?"

"I don't know," Tucker said. "Dope addicts are too complicated."

"But you shouldn't have to need to do something," Natalia said. "If you have to need to do something, and you don't do it, then you'll only do something worse."

It sounded reasonable to Tucker and not reasonable to Tucker. He decided one reason he was not sure whether or not Natalia made good sense was that he never fully concentrated on what she was saying. He was always sitting there wondering things like: did he smell of perspiration because he had on a heavy wool sweater indoors? if he took off his shoes like everyone else, would his feet smell? and was his breath all right? He had never had such thoughts before, but now he had them, and he felt like all those characters in television commercials swapping anti-odor tips with each other, except he had no one to compare notes with. Sometimes he would go into the Hockers' bathroom and raise his arms and smell his armpits, and often when he came back out he sat with his arms glued to his sides.

After Tucker left Woerner's with Dinky, they walked down to Court Street on their way to the library. In front of Chock Full O' Nuts, Dinky said, "Do you want to try out their new barbecue sauce? It has onions in it, and it's really neat."

"You try it out," Tucker said. "I'll come with you."

"I'm not going to sit at the counter if you're just going to take up space beside me. They don't like that in Chock Full O' Nuts."

"I don't know what I'd order," Tucker said, trying to find a comfortable way to carry Mrs. Hocker's four pies.

"All *right!*" Dinky said, as though she were going to have to make a big sacrifice on account of him. "I'll order two franks and you can pretend one is yours."

"How did that guy eat, anyway?" Tucker said as they went inside.

"Who?"

"The one with the cauliflower sacs on his head, whose mouth was out of line."

"Who cares how he ate?" Dinky said. "There was more to him than how he ate. Everybody thinks about how much someone eats and not about what makes someone tick!"

Tucker didn't say anything.

"Three franks," Dinky told the waitress, "and a heavenly coffee."

Then Dinky turned to Tucker and said, "She'll be back Saturday afternoon. She'll be going to St. Marie's with me. I guess she'll be around for a while."

When Tucker got home, at ten minutes to five, the martini pitcher was on the table in the living room. His uncle handed him a glass of milk.

"Come on in, Tucker, we're about to start the toasts."

His uncle's name was Guy Bell, but everyone called him Jingle, and he was not the type who minded. He was around forty. He had been divorced three times. He drove an old Rolls Royce he called Betty Boop, and Tucker's mother claimed he owed half of New York City money. He had once been an actor and now said he was a playwright, and he called people who weren't connected with theater "civilians" and spent a lot of time worrying about grants coming through to "subsidize" him.

Tucker took off his coat, after putting the milk down on the coffee table. Once he sat down, Jingle handed him the milk again.

"Isn't there any Coke?" Tucker said.

"Not for this toast," Jingle said. "Coke rots your teeth."

"Gin rots your liver," Tucker shrugged.

Tucker's mother said, "You're in that same sour mood you were in at breakfast, honey. Now try to get into the spirit of things. Your father and Jingle have an announcement to make."

The martinis were poured then. They all raised their glasses and drank to the forthcoming announcement. Then Tucker's father talked for a while.

What he said was all news to Tucker.

He started off by saying he had never really respected himself for being a professional fund raiser, and that as a professional fund raiser, he had led a dull, unrewarding life.

All Tucker could think of was the excitement that used to fill the house when Tucker's father was on the track of a "signer." In professional fund raising, the whole trick was to rope in someone very important and respectable to be the signer of all the letters which went out to people, asking for money. A Rockefeller, a Ford, someone like Edward Kennedy—these were all logical signers. People would see one of their names on a letter asking for a contribution to a hospital or a college, and they would know that it was a worthy cause.

A lot of work that didn't look like work went into getting just the right signer: golf games and lunches and telephone calls here and there, and little Sunday supper invitations, and everything Natalia would probably call "sly."

Tucker's father was always at his best in pursuit of a signer. He'd come home and give blow-by-blow descriptions of his progress to Tucker's mother. When the signer was finally in the bag, Tucker's father would take Tucker and his mother to dinner at a swanky restaurant.

"I never had any elation about what I did!"

Tucker's father was saying as he poured himself another martini. "I never had any joy about the job."

Tucker's mother made no comment, but sat with this broad smile cemented across her face, waiting for the new scheme to unfold.

Jingle said, "What Cal is trying to say is that fund raising didn't do anything for *Cal*. Sure, it did a lot for Lenox Hill, and The Lighthouse, and American Cancer, and Backwater College for Girls, but it didn't help Cal!"

Tucker finally said, "What's the new business going to be, then?"

"Health food!" Tucker's father said, raising his glass again. "Tonight we are christening a new baby called Help Yourself, Inc."

"Help Yourself!" Jingle raised his glass again. too. "Here's to a new business, a new philosophy, a whole new way of life, all wrapped up in one little combination store-restaurant."

"Where do you plan to open this place?" said Tucker's mother.

Jingle said, "Right here in Brooklyn."

"Right here in Brooklyn *Heights*," Tucker's father said.

THREE

ON SUNDAY, Tucker, Dinky, and Natalia took the IRT 7th Avenue subway to the Eastern Parkway—Brooklyn Museum station. From there they walked to the high path along the Overlook of Brooklyn Botanic Gardens. They found a bench, and the moment they sat down, Dinky took a turkey sandwich, in a Baggie, from her coat pocket.

No one said anything about the fact Dinky had just finished Sunday dinner, which was turkey with gravy, yams, string beans, biscuits, Waldorf salad, and pumpkin pie.

"This place," said Dinky, "is really something in the spring and summer." She pointed her sandwich down at the gardens and said, "In the spring and summer there are roses, lilacs, tulips, and flowering cherries. I like to bring a picnic here. We'll bring a picnic here in the spring."

Dinky was wearing jeans and a plaid flannel shirt which belonged to her father, and her father's red-and-black-wool hunter's jacket. Tucker was in old clothes, too. But Natalia was in a black velvet dress with a white lace collar, a black wool coat and a black fur hat. She wore black patent-leather shoes, and stockings, and a white angora scarf with matching mittens.

"I was glad to get out of the house, anyway," said Dinky, "even if this isn't the ideal time of year to come here."

"I like it here this time of year," Natalia said.

"So do I," said Tucker.

Dinky said, "That's because neither of you know better. You can see anything here in the summer, even more than the spring. I saw a woman nursing a baby here last summer right in the middle of the Cranford Rose Garden, and you always see kids making out on blankets down near Cherry Walk. This isn't a good time of year for the Botanic Gardens."

"People live in the past," Natalia said. " 'In the carriages of the past you can't go anywhere.' "

"That's neat," Tucker said. "Where'd you hear that?"

"It was on our bulletin board at school," Natalia said. "Maxim Gorky said it."

"What school is that?" Tucker said.

Dinky said, "I don't live in the past. I just happen to know more about the Botanic Gardens than you two, and I'm telling you this is the wrong time of year to see them!"

"It was your idea to come here," Tucker said.

Natalia said, "She wanted to get out of the house because her parents were having a disagreement."

"They were having a fight," Dinky said, "at the top of their lungs."

"Dinky's mother wants her father to defend this heroin addict," Natalia said. "The court assigned him a lawyer, but Dinky's mother said he isn't a good lawyer, not as good as Uncle Horace, anyway."

"My father's right," said Dinky. "There's nothing he can do for the guy. The guy's been shooting smack since he was thirteen. He's a recidivist in capital letters!"

"Is shooting smack taking heroin?" Tucker said.

"It's not just *taking* heroin," Dinky said, "It's wallowing in it. That guy lives to shoot up. He'd kill his grandmother for a ten-dollar bag. He'd hammer you to death for half the price of a snort."

"I like things out of season," Natalia changed the subject. "That's why I like coming here in late November."

"That guy has track marks on his ankles," Dinky said. "He's got acne everywhere, including the insides of his ears, just from being a smack-head."

"Does heroin give you pimples?" Tucker asked.

"All junk does. Junkies love sweets," Dinky said authoritatively, "I never met a junkie who didn't verge on bulbous acne."

"How can you eat and talk about bulbous acne?" Tucker said.

"I'm not finicky," Dinky answered.

She finished her sandwich and they walked from the Overlook down to the Cherry Esplanade, and across to the Oriental Garden. They talked about dope addicts, and the man Dinky was doing the book report about who had the big cauliflower sacs on his head and no hands; and they talked about dwarfs and pinheads and a woman Dinky had read about whose ears were attached to her shoulders. Dinky did most of the talking. They sat around the lake near the Oriental Garden staring up at the fir trees and ginkgoes, the mountain ashes and locusts, and Dinky passed around a 45¢-size box of Milk Duds.

"One of the strangest things I ever heard," said Dinky, "was the story of this doctor my mother knew. He specialized in hydrocephalics."

"What are they?" Tucker said.

"They're people with water on the brain. They have oversized heads. Their heads are so big they can hardly carry them on their shoulders. They don't live long."

"I've seen one of those," Natalia said.

Dinky said, "This doctor never treated anyone but hydrocephalics. They were all children whose parents brought them to him, to see if there was anything he could do. He had three normal children of his own. How he got interested in hydrocephalics is anyone's guess. That was just his thing."

"That's not so strange," Natalia said. "He just had a specialty."

"*Fermez la bouche* and let me finish," Dinky

said. "The strange part of the whole story was that his fourth child turned out to be a hydrocephalic."

"Oh wow," said Natalia.

"His wife turned into a drunk," Dinky said. "Even though it's a scientific fact you can't catch hydrocephalus, or even carry it in your genes, his wife believed that somehow his whole interest in the subject was responsible."

"That's quite a story," Tucker agreed.

"What's the strangest thing *you* ever heard, Tucker?" Natalia asked.

Tucker remembered one of the confession stories for *Stirring Romances* his mother had been working on some weeks ago. It wasn't a true story, none of the confession stories in those magazines ever were true. It was supposed to be this nurse's confession of something she had done years ago. The photograph accompanying the story showed a nurse in her white cap, sitting on a high stool, weeping, with her face buried in her hands.

Tucker said, "The strangest thing I ever heard was the story of this nurse my mother knew. She'd worked in this hospital for about twenty years, in the small town where she lived. She was very bitter because she was from a poor family, and besides that she couldn't have children of her own."

"Why couldn't she?" Dinky said.

"She just couldn't," said Tucker. "Some women can't."

"What happened?" Natalia said.

"She confessed one day that for twenty years she'd been switching newborn babies around. She'd been changing their name tags. She'd take a rich man's new baby and switch name tags with a poor man's new baby. No one in the town had the right baby. No one knew who their real brothers and sisters were, or who their real mothers and fathers were, after she made her confession twenty years later."

Dinky whistled and hit her forehead with her palm.

The title of that *Stirring Romance* story had been "I Made Their Lives a Mockery."

Natalia said, "Didn't she keep track of whose baby she was giving to who?"

"No," Tucker said. "She kept no records. She just made their lives a mockery."

Dinky said, "Probably something like that happened when I was born. That's probably why I have a gland problem and no one else in the family does. I'm probably some circus fat lady's illegitimate child."

Dinky got thirsty and the trio made their way toward Flatbush Avenue where Dinky remembered there were street vendors selling orange drinks. For a while they discussed nothing but the awful possibilities which could have resulted from the nurse's actions, and finally Tucker became aware that he and Dinky had been hogging the conversation.

"What's the strangest thing you ever heard?" he asked Natalia.

She had this funny little faraway smile, and she

just shrugged and replied, "I know a lot of strange things."

Dinky said, "One strange thing is the fact they don't sell food or refreshments of any kind in this place. They do in Central Park, in Manhattan. You can buy a whole hot meal at the cafeteria by the zoo."

"Let Natalia answer," Tucker said.

"She doesn't have to if she doesn't want to," Dinky said.

"That's all right," Natalia said.

Tucker looked from one to the other. It suddenly occurred to him that Dinky had purposely butted in every time he asked Natalia a question about herself. It suddenly dawned on him that Dinky was actually protecting Natalia in some way, and this was a side of Dinky which Tucker had never seen.

Tucker mulled it over as they walked down past the Rock Garden toward Flatbush Avenue, and he didn't say anything; no one did for a while.

Then Natalia said, "There was a boy at our school who always wore his clothes backward. He insisted on it. The teachers would make him change them around, but the minute he was out of their sight, he'd put them on backward again."

Tucker didn't ask why and neither did Dinky. There was something building up, and Tucker could feel it. Tucker's Creative-Writing teacher, Mr. Baird, would have described the feeling as "far-out vibes," meaning there were certain peculiar vibrations in the air, with no logical reason for their being there.

Then Natalia continued, "You see, until he came to our school, he was in a lot of other schools. His parents and a lot of psychologists had always thought he was a slow learner."

"Shrinks are all crazy," Dinky said. "I had to see a shrink once because of my glandular problem, and he said I ate too much because I had anger bottled up in me."

"*Some* shrinks are all right," Natalia said.

Tucker remained silent.

"I don't have any anger bottled up in me," Dinky said. "If anything, I lean the other way. Who else would take in some alley cat advertised for adoption on a tree?"

Natalia said, "This boy's name was Tony. Before he came to our school they thought he was retarded. He was going to schools where all the others were really retarded. He stopped talking and he wouldn't do anything but sit in a chair with his clothes on backward, staring at the wall. His mother was this mean woman who took out all her anger on him. *She* really did have anger bottled up in her, and she used to beat him black and blue when he was a baby. . . . Then one day he heard her say he was 'backward.' That's when he began wearing all his clothes backward."

Dinky said, "The shrinks should pay more attention to stupid mothers like that, and leave normal people with gland problems alone."

"He's okay now, though," Natalia said. "He's not even in our school anymore. He's in regular school."

"So are you now," Dinky said.

"I hope so," Natalia said.

Tucker said, "Where is this street vendor located on Flatbush Avenue?" His heart was beating very fast, and he had been unable to think of anything else to say. Then he hated himself for butting in with something about a street vendor, when obviously whatever was going on was more important than Dinky getting a cardboard carton of orange sugar water.

"I don't care if Tucker knows," Natalia said.

"I'm warning you, I've only known him about a month," Dinky said, as though Tucker wasn't there. "I only know him because Nader gave his father asthma. It's about all we have in common."

"For Pete's sake!" Tucker said.

"For Pete's sake *what?*" said Dinky. "I *don't* know you."

"That's great!" Tucker said furiously.

"I trust Tucker," Natalia said. "I don't think it'll make any difference to him that I've been in a special school."

"It doesn't make any difference at all," Tucker said.

"It's called Renaissance," Natalia said. "That means 'a new emergence.' That's where I went for Thanksgiving. Everybody at Renaissance has problems."

"You're all over yours," Dinky said.

"Mental problems," Natalia said.

"I get it," Tucker said softly.

"I hope I'm okay now," Natalia said.

"Now that you know about it," Dinky said to Tucker, "don't blab it all over Brooklyn Heights."

Tucker didn't even answer her.

"I'm not ashamed of it, if that's what you think," Natalia said. "But sometimes it's harder when everyone's looking at you for signs of something."

"Another thing," Dinky said. "When she rhymes, she's nervous. I just found that out myself, last night."

"That's true, all right," Natalia said. "True all right, crew all right, you all right, through all right—"

"Moo all night," Dinky broke in "drew all right—"

They were both laughing.

"It really does make you feel better," Dinky said.

Tucker said, "Chew all right, shoe all right, stew all night—"

"Whew! All *right!*" Natalia ended it.

"One thing still puzzles me," Dinky said when they'd stopped laughing and were almost to Flatbush Avenue.

"What's that?" said Natalia.

"How did he go to the john?"

"Who?"

"Tony. How did he go to the john with his pants on backward?"

Tucker actually blushed while the girls collapsed with laughter again.

When Tucker got back to the town house, Jingle had poster boards and poster paint spread out on the living-room floor. He was making signs for the walls of Help Yourself, chain smoking, and listening to a recording of *Carmina Burana*.

"Your mother and father are walking across Brooklyn Bridge for some exercise," Jingle told Tucker. "Sit down and listen to the music. You ought to listen to more good music. Your rock music can make you deaf, did you know that? In fact, I'm going to do a sign about that."

Several finished posters were drying across the coffee table:

BONE MEAL CAN RELIEVE ANXIETY

EACH PUFF OF A CIGARETTE COSTS 45 SECONDS OF LIFE

YOUR NERVES NEED CHOLINE

B_{12} FOR BETTER EYESIGHT

Tucker got a Coke in the kitchen and brought in a clean ashtray to replace the overflowing one at Jingle's elbow. By Jingle's own calculation, Tucker figured Jingle had used up 900 seconds of his life that afternoon alone.

"Listen to this record carefully," Jingle said. "Monks sang these songs in the 13th Century, only they're not religious songs so don't look like you're going to toss your cookies, Tucker."

"It isn't the songs," Tucker said. "It's the stale smoke."

"Listen!" Jingle said, and then Jingle translated the words after the chorus sang them. " 'Pretty is thy face,/the look of thine eyes,/the braids of thy hair; o how beautiful thou art!' "

Tucker was just beginning to get interested when Jingle added, "For a young man in love, you have no soul, Tucker. Now *this* is a love song. This has poetry, Tucker."

"Who said I was in love?" Tucker said. "I don't happen to be."

His tone of voice, like Jingle's posters, didn't carry a lot of conviction.

On the other hand, his pulse was normal, he slept well most nights, and he didn't think of her *all* the time.

He had some of the symptoms, he allowed . . . but not the actual disease.

FOUR

THE FIRST day of December, all over Tucker's school, mimeographed notices announced:

LET'S HEAR IT FOR THE FIFTIES!
DRESS UP, DANCE, AND DO IT LIKE
THEY DID IN THE 1950'S.
SONGS FROM THE FIFTIES—LIVE!
REFRESHMENTS!
FRIDAY, DECEMBER 10, IN THE RICHTER
SCHOOL GYM; 8 O'CLOCK AT NIGHT.
$1.00 Single; $1.50 with date.

Tucker took down one of the notices and wrote

across the bottom: *Natalia, want to go to this with me? T.*

The next afternoon while Dinky, Natalia, and Tucker were watching the 4:30 movie over at the Hockers', Tucker passed her the note when Dinky wasn't looking. Natalia took it into the bathroom to read, and Tucker tried to exercise Nader by throwing a balled-up empty pack of Kent cigarettes for her to retrieve. Dinky's eyes were glued to *I Died A Thousand Times,* starring Jack Palance and Shelley Winters. She was working her way through a box of Hydrox cookies.

When Natalia returned, she had written something under Tucker's invitation.

I'll go if Dinky has a date for it too.

To Tucker's mind, that was like Natalia saying she'd go if it snowed for three months straight in Biloxi, Mississippi, or if all the Republican members of Congress asked for asylum in Russia.

Tucker Woolf had never had a date in his life, and besides feeling the unfairness of Natalia's demand, he felt relief. He gave a shrug of his shoulders across the room in Natalia's direction, as if to say, "Well, that's the way the ball bounces, old girl."

Then the following day, P. John Knight got up in Creative Writing to read his poem called "Thanks to the United Nations."

P. John Knight was not a popular character at Richter School.

The poem he stood up to read said a lot about P. John.

Aren't you glad the Chinese are in the U.N. now?
Oh boy! And how!
Who wants to live forever?
Do you? Do I? Welcome, slant-eye.
Aren't you glad we'll wake up in our beds,
Someday taken over by the Reds?
Who are also Yellow?
Give a Chinese cheer: Chop!
Give a cheer: Hip!
Give a Chinese boo: Suey!
Give a boo: Phooey!
Give a two-timing U.N. cheer:
Hip phooey! Chop suey! Yea!

"Well," said Mr. Baird, the instructor, when P. John sat down, "That's more politics than poetry."

"All great poets mix politics with poetry," P. John said, "Yevtushenko, Joel Oppenheimer, Pablo Neruda."

"Who's Pablo Neruda?" Mr. Baird asked.

P. John heaved an exasperated sigh. "He *only* won the Nobel Prize for 1971, Professor!"

You had to hand it to P. John: he *did* know his facts.

Mr. Baird said, "But *your* politics overwhelm your poetry."

"Nobody ever thinks so when a pinko puts anti-

American sentiments into a poem," said P. John. "My politics just aren't your politics."

The truth was, P. John's politics weren't like anyone else's at Richter School, and P. John himself wasn't much like anyone in the school. He had a real old-fashioned haircut, nearly as short as a Marine boot's, and he always wore double-breasted suits, old-style button-down shirts, and striped neckties. He *was* a year older than most of the students, but at sixteen he looked middle-aged.

But it was not the way P. John dressed, and it was not P. John's poem, which suddenly drew Tucker's attention that afternoon in Creative Writing. It was something so basic about P. John that Tucker would have been inclined to ignore it altogether, if it hadn't been for the Fifties dance.

P. John Knight was a fat boy. He was nearly six feet, with red hair, freckles and red-apple cheeks, and he weighed around 220 pounds.

"Wait up!" Tucker yelled at P. John after class.

P. John looked around surprised, with a *who, me?* expression on his face. No one at Richter went out of his way to walk with P. John.

"That was an interesting poem, P. John," Tucker said.

"How come you didn't write one?"

"I didn't finish it," Tucker said.

"No one in this place is very diligent," P. John said, "What was your unfinished poem about?"

Tucker wasn't sure how P. John would react to his giving thanks for the library in Brooklyn

Heights, so he said, "It was about Brooklyn Heights. I just moved over there."

P. John said, "People who live in Brooklyn Heights never say they live in Brooklyn, do they? They always say Brooklyn Heights so nobody will think they're commoners." P. John laughed wisely and shook his head as though there was no end to the folly of the human race.

"You know too much for your own good, P. John," Tucker began buttering him up. "That's why everyone envies you."

" 'Whoever envies another,' " P. John said, " 'secretly allows that person's superiority.' Horace Walpole wrote that, and it's true."

"What does it mean?" Tucker said.

"Well, for instance, everyone around here allows me to be superior, so I'll take up all the class time reading my work. That way it's never discovered that nobody else did his work."

"All work and no play makes Jack miss the Fifties dance," said Tucker.

"Are you selling tickets?"

"I'm just trying to locate a superior person to escort a friend of mine," Tucker said.

"Who are *you* escorting?"

"A friend of hers."

"I see," P. John said.

"We could double date."

"Why *me?*" P. John said.

"This girl reads a lot. She just finished this book about this man in Victorian England. Ashley Montagu wrote it," Tucker said.

"*What* man? *What* book?"

"I can't exactly remember."

"This girl sounds like she needs to be rescued from her inattentive peers, if you're an accurate sampling of her peer group."

"I am," Tucker said. "I don't remember things down to a fine point."

P. John stopped and removed a small leather notebook from his coat pocket.

"Can you remember her name and address?"

On the night of December 10th, P. John appeared at the Joralemon Street town house promptly at 7:30.

Tucker's father and Jingle were in the living room going over a shipment of rose-hip Vitamin C tablets, Chew-C-Vites, Herb Blend Tea, Papaya Liquid Cleansing Cream, et cetera. Tucker's mother was darting around in the background trying out yogurt makers and food choppers.

Jingle explained Help Yourself to P. John, and P. John nodded hs head in that old wiser-than-all-the-world way and said, "You'll probably attract a lot of radicals."

"Just what does *that* mean?" Tucker's father looked up from a carton of Wheat Germ Oil Caps with a cranky frown on his forehead. His new business venture had done nothing to improve his mood. He was beginning to take all the health-food literature very seriously. He had cut out coffee, substituting papaya-mint tea, so that breakfast with him was like eating next to someone with all the symptoms on the side of a Compōz box.

P. John answered, "It's just that a lot of radicals are health nuts and vegetarians. Hitler was. George Bernard Shaw was. Hitler's the exception, though. Most of them are weak-sister socialists like Shaw."

"I suppose you prefer Hitler?" Tucker's father said.

"To Shaw? Certainly. I don't agree with him all the way down the line, but he didn't cozy up to the Communists like a lot of jelly-spined liberals."

"You're a pretty opinionated fellow," Tucker's father said.

"I have a few solid opinions," P. John agreed. "Law and order. Better dead than red. If you outlaw guns, only outlaws will own guns. . . . Clichés, for the sake of summary."

"Oh spare me, spare me, spare me," Jingle said, "from women with hard hearts, and men with hard hats, and things that go bump in the night."

Behind P. John's back, Jingle raised his eyes to the ceiling as though he thought he'd seen everything until Tucker had waltzed in with this weirdo.

When they arrived at the Hockers', both Mr. and Mrs. Hocker met them at the door, like the First Family on the White House steps greeting guests for a state dinner.

"The girls will be out in a minute," Mr. Hocker said. "They're to be home by twelve. Let's all check our watches now."

"I don't own a watch anymore," P. John said. "A mugger relieved me of it in September, no doubt so he could report to the unemployment office in time to sign for his check."

Mr. Hocker bit his lip and stared thoughtfully at P. John.

"I have a watch," Tucker said. They synchronized their watches and Mr. Hocker said, "I don't want them riding back on the subway." He shoved a five-dollar bill at P. John for cab fare.

P. John handed it back. "I'm one of your few New Yorkers not on the dole."

Mrs. Hocker said nervously, "It sounds like fun, this dance, but I bet neither of you boys remembers the fifties."

"One of my heroes is from the fifties," P. John said. "Senator Joseph R. McCarthy, the great crusader against Communism."

Mrs. Hocker swallowed hard, and Mr. Hocker barked, "He wasn't one of *our* heroes. He was a misinformed, insensitive, trouble-making headline grabber."

For a minute no one could think of anything to say, and then Tucker shrugged helplessly and managed, "That's what makes horse races, I guess."

The girls appeared. Dinky was wearing a beige dress which looked like a huge feed bag someone had cut armholes in, and Natalia was wearing velvet again, light blue with gold buttons down the front.

"This is P. John Knight, Dinky," said Tucker. "P. John, this is Dinky."

Dinky said, "What's the P. stand for?"

50

"Perry," said P. John. "It's my father's name, so I don't use it."

"That saves confusion," Dinky said.

"Exactly," P. John answered. "I don't like to be confused with anyone."

"Natalia," Tucker said, "This is P. John. P. John, this is Natalia Line."

"How do you do," P. John said, and then he turned back to Dinky. "You must have another name besides Dinky."

"It's Susan," Dinky said.

Mrs. Hocker said, "Dinky is our affectionate name for her."

P. John held his arm out as though Dinky were his partner for the grand march at the beginning of a fancy dress ball. "Shall we be off, Susan?"

Dinky was busy buttoning her coat, but she stopped as if on command, and took P. John's arm.

It was a majestic beginning as they strode toward the door like royalty, with Natalia and Tucker following behind. But there was no way for the two of them to fit in one doorway. There was a moment of awkwardness, as Dinky dropped behind to let P. John precede her.

P. John kept saying, "After you, after you," until finally Dinky went first. Then things became more confused as P. John also waited for Natalia to go ahead of him. He kept saying "Ladies first," and "After you," the sort of thing parents would approve of. But when Tucker glanced over his shoulder, as they went down the steps, both the Hockers were standing there frowning, waving good-bye with doubtful expressions.

Tucker wasn't really sure what their expressions meant. Dinky clarified things as they all walked down Remsen Street toward the subway.

"You couldn't have known it," she said to P. John, "but one of my father's pet hates was that Senator Joe McCarthy."

"It wouldn't have made any difference if I *had* known it," said P. John. "A man has to speak his mind, Susan."

"Well, Natalia," said Tucker, beginning his own little conversation as they walked behind Dinky and P. John, "How's every little thing?" But he didn't hear her answer. He was thinking that he had never once in his life referred to himself as a man, as P. John just had. He was also thinking that he couldn't dance well, make conversation easily on a date with anyone as attractive as Natalia Line, or do anything suave, confident, or even polite. He couldn't even hold out his arm for Natalia to take. It was like his arm was paralyzed. He was obviously not ready for this first date, and he wouldn't have minded breaking his leg or coming down with appendicitis on the spot.

Natalia was walking beside him silently, that self-conscious kind of silence between two people when both brains are shrieking: say something about the weather, say something about a movie you saw, or a book you read, or something, anything, hurry, do it, *talk!* . . . but the tongues could care less.

So much for fixing up a pair of fatties out of the kindness of your heart Tucker thought; the fatties didn't need any favors.

He was glad when they got down into the subway and began the rattle-banging trip under the East River into New York, because then you couldn't hear anything anyone said, anyway.

The whole affair was a nerve-wrecking fiasco where Tucker was concerned. He spent it under huge photographs of Johnny Ray and scenes from *A Streetcar Named Desire,* and pictures of Howdy Doody and The Mousketeers, wiping off his palms on his handkerchief, and stepping all over Natalia's patent-leather shoes. The more he became aware that he was a failure on the dating scene, the more obnoxious and bumptious he seemed to become.

Once, when he was dancing close to Natalia while the orchestra was playing, "Hey there, you with the stars in your eyes, love never made a fool of you, you used to be too wise," he began to feel really moved, and then self-conscious about breathing with his mouth so close to her ear. He began to fear he was breathing hotly down her neck, the way sex maniacs did in the confession stories his mother edited, and he tried to stop breathing until the song was finished. This produced a coughing attack so bad it brought tears to his eyes, and they had to leave the dance floor.

Natalia did not say anything to make him feel better. She just stood meekly beside him on the sidelines while he wiped his eyes and blew his nose. He told her that conceivably he could have a touch of asthma like his father. She said a lot of people who had asthma really had terrible anxieties which made it all worse. Tucker decided the thing wrong was that they were both "inadequates." They were not ready for the social scene.

Then, too, the thing he had never known about the fifties was that all the popular songs were really sentimental and romantic.

He tried to blot out the lyrics by making himself remember all the words to old Beatle hits like "Eleanor Rigby" and "Lucy in the Sky with Diamonds." But the lead singer had a microphone, and the words to the songs filled the room; there was no escaping them. There was "I Need You Now," and "Hello, Young Lovers," and "Getting To Know You," and "Too Young."

Tucker was also trying to dance without moving his arms very much. He had smelled his armpits in the john and he was perspiring, all right, worse than a Rose Bowl tackle on New Year's Day.

Every time Tucker looked up, he seemed to see Dinky and P. John gliding by like the Sweetheart Couple at the Valentine Ball. They didn't even look fat anymore.

Only yesterday, Tucker had expected P. John to get him aside at some point during the evening, and chew him out for suckering him into a date with Dinky. But when they met in the john near the end of the evening, P. John said to Tucker,

"Susan's got a mind like a steel trap. She's okay!"

Tucker had never given any thought to Dinky's mind. It was not the main thing the average person meeting Dinky noticed.

Tucker said, "She can really move around for someone that heavy."

"She's going to start attending Weight Watchers with me," P. John said. "It helps when someone goes with you."

"Well, she's the ideal one to accompany you," Tucker answered. "No offense intended."

"Susan and I aren't sensitive about our weight," P. John said. "We're just realistic about the hard work ahead, getting down to normal. This is the last night we'll indulge ourselves."

The end of the evening was sort of like an average couple out on the town with the two Most Populars in the senior class. They all went to Burg-a-Cue on 20th and Third after the dance. While Dinky and P. John cracked jokes and exchanged clever remarks, devouring heaps of french fries and hamburgers, Tucker and Natalia had this really boring conversation about all the bad things restaurants did to food. That, mixed in with the sight of Dinky's and P. John's mouths, which were never closed and always full of things being ground up by their teeth and swallowed, also took away Tucker's appetite.

He began pushing the food around on his plate, to make it look like he'd eaten more than he had. Natalia had finished a hamburger way before anyone else, because she had hardly said anything besides: "I've heard they grind up horsemeat for hot-dog stuffing."

"Not horsemeat. Pigs' intestines," Tucker had replied, which was just a sample of their brilliant repartee.

Tucker supposed Natalia was afraid to say much of anything, for fear she'd rhyme. It was possible, too, that she was too bored even to rhyme.

They took a taxi back to the Heights, and Tucker sat up front with the driver. There was hardly enough room in back for Natalia. Dinky and P. John had her squeezed into the side of the taxi door.

P. John kept leaning forward to see Tucker's watch. He kept telling Dinky he'd better get her home on time, since he hadn't made a very good first impression on her father.

"Just don't tell him any of your opinions," Dinky said. "He happens to be a very big liberal."

They made it exactly on the dot of twelve. Mr. Hocker was in the doorway as they brought the girls up the steps.

"Good night, boys," he said very pointedly. There was no lingering.

At the corner of Remsen and Henry, while Tucker was saying good night to P. John, P. John said, "Let's do it again, sometime."

"Sure thing," Tucker said but the likelihood of his ever going through an evening like that again was about as sure a thing as hot snow falling or cold water boiling.

FIVE

THE MORNING after the dance, instead of sleeping late as he always did on Saturday mornings, Tucker was up at six thirty.

He sat around in the living room in his pajamas, listening to old records, and trying to make sense out of some poetry written by this Sylvia Plath. She had killed herself when she was very young. Everyone in Tucker's Creative Writing class was carrying around *Ariel*, and raving over lines like:

I should sit on a rock off Cornwall and comb my hair.
I should wear tiger pants, I should have an affair.
We should meet in another life, we should meet in air,
Me and you.

57

Last night when he was trying to sleep in the face of flashes of everything he had done wrong on his date with Natalia, he had finally decided to just never see her again: to begin a whole new life as though she'd never existed.

He had made a mental list of new interests he was going to become involved in: astronomy, tennis, chess, and carpentry; and he doubted he'd have any time left over for girls and dances.

Jingle came by about eight in the morning. Tucker's parents were still asleep, so Tucker offered to help Jingle carry down some supplies to the store on Montague Street which was going to house Help Yourself.

"I suppose you heard your father and I had a fight last night," said Jingle.

Tucker nodded. He was glad that it had happened. When he'd gotten in, his father and mother were too busy discussing the argument to question Tucker about his date.

The trouble had started when Jingle wanted to hang blow-ups of people like Mae West and Greta Garbo on the walls of Help Yourself. Jingle said they were good examples of health-food followers. Tucker's father complained that Jingle wasn't taking the business seriously enough, and that Jingle was confusing it with show business.

"The trouble with your father is that he has no real style," Jingle said. "Do you know what I mean, Tucker?"

"Sort of," Tucker said. Tucker's mother sometimes called his father and him her "two dark

58

clouds" because they never laughed at anything on television and they never liked flashy ties she picked out for them at Christmas. Jingle loved her taste in ties and he always bent double watching the boob-tube comedies.

"Your father doesn't know how to dress up a sentence, or dress himself up, or dress up a business and make it have a little pizazz," Jingle said. "He thinks it's enough to just *be* there in life."

"It's not, though," Tucker said. He had learned that lesson the hard way on his date with Natalia.

"You bet your tiny little behind it's not!" Jingle said. "A boy has to hustle in this world."

"Who won the argument?" Tucker said.

"Your father has a 70% interest, and I only have a 30% interest," Jingle said. "So your father will probably get his way. The walls of Help Yourself will be as colorful as a sack of flour."

"I didn't know things were that uneven," Tucker said. "70—30, that's really uneven."

"You know how your father is with money. He squirrels it," Jingle said. "Did you ever know your father to really splurge on anything, like a *Patek Phillipe* watch, or a weekend ski trip to Switzerland?"

"He doesn't ski," Tucker said.

"Don't be dense," Jingle said. "You know what I mean. My sister has no jewels! One diamond the size of a *petit pois* and *that's it!*"

Tucker said, "My mother says big rocks are vulgar."

"What else *could* she say?" Jingle said. "She could hardly say I'd like to rip up my whole life in little pieces and start all over again, could she?"

"I guess my father's fairly conservative," Tucker said.

"Which is all right in the fund-raising business," Jingle said, "but in this business it's going to be our *bête noire*."

Over the weekend, Tucker's father began experimenting with health-food recipes. For Sunday breakfast there was Granola Cereal Mix, made with soy flour and unsulphured dates, and wheat germ, sesame seed and raw honey. For Sunday lunch, eggplant cutlet with organically-grown vegetables in sour cream. Supper was haddock salad and Ambrosia Cream.

Monday morning, Tucker's mother made a date with him for that night in New York, for dinner and Christmas shopping. Tucker was to meet her outside the Donnell Library after she finished work at 5:30.

Tucker didn't go back to Brooklyn Heights after school. During school he avoided P. John, which was easy, because the Creative Writing class didn't meet Mondays. Tucker was still sticking to the idea of putting Natalia and Dinky and that evening out of his mind. He had already signed up for shop next term, and inquired when the chess club met.

At 3:30 he caught the Third Avenue bus up to

the fifties and walked across to Donnell Library, with every intention of investigating books on astronomy.

There were librarians and librarians. There were the ones who wrote letters and read the latest magazines behind the information desks, and looked up at you as though you'd just dropped into their living rooms uninvited. And there were the ones who conducted a small inquisition before getting up from their seats: *Is it listed in the card catalog; did you look for it in the 600 section; did you look in Pay Duplicate?*

But always, Tucker knew, there were the ones who really really knew where everything was, and the answer to every conceivable question, and ways to look up things which would shame and astonish Socrates, Plato, Solomon and Dr. Pangloss.

Such a librarian was on duty that afternoon in Donnell, behind the desk in the third floor reference room.

In minutes she produced a large blue volume with a paragraph in it, summing up the information Tucker had requested.

Renaissance House: For emotionally disturbed youngsters ages 11-17. Specialists with schizophrenics, as well as milder problems. Resident therapy supervision; six psychologists on staff and consulting psychiatrist. Year-round academic classes in all subjects. Excellent music, art, and physical ed. program on 500 acre estate, cottage plan. Limited enrollment. Box 12, Doylestown, Pa.

Tucker sat there thinking for a while after he finished the paragraph. He began to nail-bite, which was a throwback to his younger days when he attended public school on the West Side in New York and gangs of boys would mug him for his lunch money, or steal his bike out from under him; and he began to loathe himself all over again for thinking it was enough to just *be* there in life, as Jingle had pointed out his father did.

If he had had any pizazz he would have made her laugh all that evening, and made P. John ride up in front with the driver on the way home in the taxi, and held both her hand and Dinky's, and asked her for a second date, and said some great thing before kissing her good night.

There was an old man in a shabby coat sitting next to Tucker, following the words in an encyclopedia with a gnarled finger and whispering them as he read. He had a grease-stained brown paper bag next to a red cap with ear muffs attached to it, and he smelled of salami and looked like the type who lived in one of those single rooms you could look up and see him walking around in, under a naked light bulb dangling from the ceiling, with milk cartons on the window sill.

Tucker decided it was probably the way he himself would end up one day, still a library freak, still an "inadequate" with perspiring palms and underarm odor.

Before Tucker went downstairs to meet his mother, he made a photostat of an article he found in *Science Digest,* about a four-year-old girl who developed breasts and pubic hair after eating several jars of her mother's hormone cream for wrinkles. Since he would not be seeing Dinky again if he could help it, he would slip it in the mail to her. It was Dinky's kind of story.

"I think we both deserve a good thick sirloin steak," Tucker's mother said, not even bothering to study the menu in Mario's Villa d'Este, "and I need a very dry martini."

"What was your first date like with Dad?" Tucker asked while they waited for the waiter to come to the table.

"My first date with your father was ruined by Jingle," his mother said, "just as I suspect Jingle is going to ruin our future."

"Why is he going to ruin our future?"

"Because Jingle isn't really capable of being committed to anything. Jingle likes beginnings, but he doesn't like middles, and he doesn't stick around for endings. Jingle likes splash and fanfares and grand openings, but he runs from any kind of routine."

"How did he ruin your first date with Dad?" Tucker said.

"It was a double date," Tucker's mother said.

"Jingle told your father to get tickets for the theater. The stock market had fallen very low, and your father was depressed because he'd just put money into the market for the first time. But Jingle said the only way to handle that kind of depression was to defy Fate and celebrate." His mother paused to give their order to the waiter, and then she continued. "So we celebrated. Theater, dinner after at the Algonquin, and from there to Greenwich Village to hear some jazz. It was all great fun, a million yaks, except for one thing."

"What was that?" Tucker said.

"Jingle didn't have one cent. Not with him, and not in his checkbook. The whole evening was on your father. . . . *That* was our first date."

"At least what went wrong was somebody else's fault," said Tucker. "At least Dad wasn't to blame."

"Why do you say that?" his mother asked.

"No reason," Tucker shrugged. "Can I buy a tennis racket?"

"You cannot," his mother said, "but you *may*."

SIX

THERE WAS a red velvet couch shaped like a sleigh in the middle of the floor.

"I want your honest opinion about something," Tucker's father told him. It was Wednesday afternoon. Tucker had dropped into Help Yourself to see how the place was shaping up.

Jingle said, "And say what you think, Tucker. Remember our discussion about style the other morning."

Tucker set down his book bag and took off his gloves and his cap.

Jingle stretched out on the sleigh bed, lighting a Kent and smoking it through a long ivory holder.

"Tucker," his father said, "if you were going into a health-food store, would you like it to look like a clean, modern, but quaint soda shop . . . or would you like it to look like an old, dusty-type antique shop?"

"Dear God!" Jingle groaned, *"Try* to pose the question fairly, Cal!"

"Tucker," Tucker's father said, "do you think this piece of furniture your uncle is reclining on should be in a health-food store?"

"Tucker, don't answer that," Jingle said, "until I tell you that I plan to do a whole wall in red velvet, with a Tiffany lamp hanging from the ceiling and this divine bed against the wall. People can just toddle over and rest their footsies while they're tossing back a Tiger's Milk. Do you see what I mean?"

"Well, Tucker?" said Tucker's father.

"I don't know," Tucker said. "I'm not good at interior decorating."

Tucker's father said, "Would *you* toddle over and rest your footsies on that piece of furniture, or would you rather sit at a nice clean fountain?"

"I'd probably sit at a fountain," Tucker said, "but I lack pizazz."

"Your uncle's going to have this place looking like a bordello!" said Tucker's father.

"What's that?" Tucker said.

"It's a place where gracious ladies sell their favors to bashful gentlemen," Jingle said.

"It's a place where ignorant women sell themselves to desperate men," said Tucker's father.

"That's all in your viewpoint," Jingle said.

"You mean a whorehouse," Tucker said. "I get it."

"This sleigh bed is my inspiration couch," Jingle said. "It's always brought me luck."

"With the kind of luck it's brought you, you should sell it for junk," said Tucker's father.

"*I* have never been dismissed from a job," said Jingle.

"You never held a job long enough to be canned," said Tucker's father.

The fight was on.

Tucker mumbled something about having homework to do and left.

He walked down Montague Street toward the East River, to the Promenade, which was built over the highway and looked out at the river and the harbor. There were benches where you could sit and think and stare at the Statue of Liberty in the distance. You could also see the big freighters docked in their berths, the Staten Island ferry making its runs, and a whole panorama of lower Manhattan.

Tucker sat down and took out his sketchbook. He was going to draw the view of Wall Street, but when his Pentel touched the paper, the sleigh bed began taking shape. He drew a mouth on the sleigh bed, and a balloon above it. He was going to show the sleigh bed ordering a Tiger's Milk, the way Jingle ordered martinis in restaurants: *I'll have a Tiger's Milk as dry as a poor beached whale, with a teensy twist of lemon, over one lonesome and anxiety-ridden ice cube.*

He had barely printed the words "I'll have" when a voice behind him said, "I'll have a seat?"

He looked around and saw Natalia. She was wearing the official St. Marie's beret, and a camel's-hair coat like all the St. Marie's girls wore.

"Sure. Have a seat," he said.

She sat down beside him, and he said, "I was sketching a cartoon."

"A cartoon you'll finish soon," she said.

"Yeah," he said, aware that she was rhyming.

He said, "I was going to call."

"You didn't call at all."

"I would have," he said.

"You could have," she said. He was wondering if he was obliged to go along with it and say, "I should have" until they were all rhymed out. But he didn't. He just sat trying to think why it was they couldn't talk together anymore, and if it was his fault or hers.

They pretended a great, silent interest in the river. Then Natalia took the Pentel from his hand and wrote something in his sketchbook.

She handed it back to him. She'd drawn a balloon with the words "I'd like to—" inside it. Now she was waiting for Tucker to finish the sentence, smiling at him with her bright eyes, pleased with this little game which Tucker's cartoon had inspired.

Tucker wrote, "be able to make conversation."

She laughed and nodded her head up and down.

Then Tucker drew another balloon and wrote inside, "I've been thinking about—" and passed the sketchbook to her.

Natalia thought a moment and wrote, "lonely times when you're laughing because you're supposed to. It makes your face hurt."

Tucker nodded. That was exactly what happened when Jingle was at a party, cracking jokes and wearing everyone out with his witticisms. Tucker's mother always said that Jingle wasn't funny—he was hysterical; the difference was you could relax around a funny person. Around Jingle sometimes your sides began to ache soon from laughing, and then no matter what he said it was a strain to keep reacting the same way. You began to wish he'd turn himself off, or someone would just pull his plug.

Natalia drew another balloon with these words inside: "We should—"

Then Tucker really cheated. He pretended to be thinking. What he was really doing was remembering parts of that Sylvia Plath poem he'd read over the weekend.

After a few seconds he wrote, "meet in another life. We should meet in air. Me and you."

When Natalia read what he'd written, she drew in her breath and looked at him, and actually spoke. "Oh that's beautiful."

"It's just a thought that came to my mind," Tucker answered.

So what if he hadn't said it wasn't *his* thought: it got Natalia talking. She didn't say a lot, but she didn't rhyme, either. And she did invite him over to the Hockers' that Friday night, for a demonstration Mrs. Hocker's Encounter Group was giving.

In the middle of an all-vegetarian dinner on Friday night, some old business acquaintance of Tucker's father called to tell him about a position opening up in the fund-raising field.

Tucker's father kept saying, "No . . . no . . . I'm afraid not . . . I don't think so," while Tucker's mother tried sign language first, and then scribbled across a piece of paper, "Tell him you'll *consider* it."

When Tucker's father put down the phone, Tucker's mother wailed, "Cal, why didn't you at least say you'd *consider* it?"

"Because I couldn't think with you waving your hands at me that way!" Tucker's father snapped.

"It sounds like such a good opportunity, Cal."

"It's not *that* good," Tucker's father said. "Let me fill you in on all the details."

That delayed dessert a good half hour. Because the whole discussion seemed too important for Tucker to interrupt, he sat it out, and he was forty minutes late getting over to the Hockers'.

P. John answered the doorbell.

"What's all that noise?" Tucker asked.

"Junkies being reborn," said P. John. "You won't believe it."

"Where's Natalia?" Tucker said.

"She's trapped between Susan's parents."

Mrs. Hocker had folding chairs set up in a circle around the living room, for guests. The members of her Encounter Group were lying in prone positions on the Oriental rug. Tucker saw the Hockers and Natalia at the center of the circle; Dinky was at the end.

There was silence in the room as Tucker and P. John sat down at the other end of the circle.

Then one of the bodies on the rug began to twitch slightly. The body belonged to a short black-haired boy whose eyes were closed; his thumb was in his mouth. First his legs jerked. Then he began whimpering. Then he rolled over on his side and drew his knees up to his chest.

He pulled his thumb out of his mouth and said, "It's so dark. I'm afraid in here."

P. John whispered to Tucker, "He's supposed to be in the womb."

"In what room?" Tucker whispered back.

"In his mother's *womb!*" P. John said.

Mrs. Hocker said, "Quiet, please. Go on, Marcus."

"I'm afraid of everything," Marcus continued. "I am afraid to stay and more afraid to go out into the world. I don't think I can. . . . I can't."

"Oh, yes, you can," Mrs. Hocker said softly. "We want you in the world."

"You do?" Marcus said. He began to whimper again. "No, no, no."

"We want you in our world, Marcus," Mrs. Hocker said. "We love you."

Mr. Hocker was sitting in the center of the room with his palm gripping his mouth, frowning.

Natalia was beside him, staring down at her patent-leather shoes as though there was something highly interesting reflected in the shine. Dinky sat at the far end of the circle chewing gum and jiggling one knee compulsively.

Then Marcus rolled over on his stomach, stretched out, and began flailing clenched fists, banging the floor with his feet, and making the noise of a baby crying.

"Good!" Mrs. Hocker was encouraging him. "Good, Marcus. Beautiful."

Marcus wailed louder.

"He's here now. He's born," Mrs. Hocker said. "Somebody slap his behind."

P. John got up to oblige.

"*Gently,* P. John!" Mrs. Hocker said.

When the next to last junkie was in the process of being reborn, Tucker went to the kitchen with P. John to help him serve the food. P. John pointed to some bowls in the refrigerator and said, "Those go on a separate tray. They're just for Susan and me."

Scotch-taped to the bowls were pieces of paper with LEGAL written across them.

"Weight Watchers separate food into legal and illegal," P. John said. "Susan and I eat only legal food."

The illegal food was overstuffed sandwiches on rye bread. The legal food was celery stalks with pimento strips across them; broiled mushrooms served cold on a bed of watercress; cucumber slices with dill sprigs; carrot sticks; radishes; sliced apples with cheese chunks attached on toothpicks; and chilled cherry tomatoes.

"The legal food looks better than the illegal food," Tucker said.

"Our food always looks and tastes better. You can't have any, though, sorry."

"I just ate," Tucker said, "but thanks, anyway."

"I don't mean to sound cold-blooded," P. John said, "but there's only enough for Susan and me. She's lost five pounds already."

"What happened to her glandular problem?" Tucker said.

"There's no such thing! Her parents never should have encouraged that idea."

"Maybe they didn't know any better," Tucker said.

"They should have made it their business to find out," P. John said. "The trouble with fat kids is they're too good-natured. No one thinks they have any problems besides eating too much. If Susan had begun carrying off the family possessions to hock shops to pay for her habit, they might have paid some attention."

"She said she saw a psychologist once," Tucker said.

"She did," P. John agreed. "Once. . . . Those smack-heads in the other room have therapy all week long, and Mrs. Hocker spends every Friday night helping them understand their problems."

"They're more complicated, I guess," Tucker said.

"They just make more waves," P. John said. "Do you know Marcus is twenty-two years old?"

Mrs. Hocker came into the kitchen as the pair were preparing to carry in the trays of food.

"P. John," she said, "if you're going to join in the discussion period, remember to be kind. You know nothing at all about Rebirth Therapy. If you can't be kind, be silent."

"I have nothing to discuss with them," P. John said. "My outlook on life is light years away from their outlook on life."

"You don't know anything about their outlook on life, either," she said.

"I know enough about their outlook to keep my money in my sock," said P. John.

"How nice to see you again, Tucker," Mrs. Hocker said, turning her back on P. John. "You're being so good about paying attention to Natalia."

"Maybe he just *wants* to pay attention to her," P. John said.

"I do," Tucker said.

"P. John," Mrs. Hocker said, "you're a very brash young man. You do test people's patience."

"I just say what I think, Ma'am."

"I hope Dinky doesn't pick up that habit," Mrs. Hocker said. "It's not a very attractive habit for a young person."

"Dinky's not a very attractive name for a young person," said P. John.

74

Mrs. Hocker didn't answer. She was getting ice trays from the refrigerator.

When her hands were full, she suddenly whirled around and kicked the door shut like a punter going for pigskin, with such force the glasses on the kitchen shelves shook.

There was so much noise and movement in the front of the house that Nader hid under the bed in Dinky's room.

Tucker went back to see her, after trying and failing to make conversation with Natalia. When Tucker last saw Natalia she was cornered by Marcus, who was shoveling down egg-salad sandwiches and reminiscing fondly about the highs he used to get on heroin before he was rehabilitated. Marcus would punctuate every paragraph with, "But don't get me wrong, man, my head was messed up."

Maybe it was Tucker's imagination, but Nader looked thinner, and seemed to have back some of her old energy.

Dinky definitely looked thinner, and Tucker had noticed another change in her. When he had passed her the photostat of the newspaper clipping about the four-year-old baby who ate her mother's hormone cream and grew breasts, Dinky read it expressionlessly.

Then Dinky said to him, "I'm not interested in the bizarre anymore."

"How come?"

"I've got to think about myself. I've got to concentrate on getting off all this blubber."

"Can't you do both?" Tucker asked.

"I've got to read more," Dinky answered. "P. John has read all of Kurt Vonnegut, Jr., except a few stories in *Welcome to the Monkey House.*"

"I only read *God Bless You, Mr. Rosewater,*" Tucker said. "But I wouldn't think P. John would like Vonnegut."

"He likes him because he's a self-made man," Dinky said. "He says you'd never find Kurt Vonnegut, Jr., on welfare."

After Tucker had petted Nader for a while and listened to a little of a new record album, he saw Natalia standing in the doorway. She had her old mischievous grin on her face, and her hands were behind her back.

"Come on in," Tucker said. "How's the discussion going?"

Natalia made a face. Then she produced a spiral notebook folded open to a page, with a balloon drawn on it.

Inside the balloon were the words "If I could be reborn, I'd be a—"

Tucker picked up a pencil and finished the sentence, "Aries instead of a Pisces, because Pisces are wishy-washy and Aries are dynamic."

"I'd be a Gemini, instead of a Libra," Natalia said, "because Geminis have two ways of looking at things."

"That makes them two-faced," Tucker said.

"No, it doesn't," Natalia said, "because they're not really one person. They're twins in one person."

"I don't know much about astrology," Tucker said, "just that Pisces are wishy-washy and Aries are dynamic. My mother's Aries. She has a really good mind." He felt relieved because they were actually beginning a conversation, but then Natalia drew another balloon and passed it to him for his turn. At first, Tucker felt self-conscious playing the Balloon Game again. There was something weird about sitting in the same room alone with a girl, passing a notebook back and forth and writing down things without speaking. But after a while there was not anything he would rather do.

The hi-fi was playing softly in the background. Nader was curled up asleep inside one of the guest's coats. A light snow was beginning to fall outside—Tucker could see it in the lamplight through the window.

And once, in answer to Tucker's question: "I think Tucker Woolf is—," Natalia had written inside the balloon, "fishing for a compliment."

Which made them both laugh, and was the only way, really, to handle it: not to let it get heavy.

When they became aware of the shouting in the living room, they thought it was another rebirth.

"It's not, though," Natalia said after she listened for a second. "It's Marcus, and he was already reborn earlier."

"Then it's probably the discussion period," Tucker said.

"It doesn't sound much like a discussion."

Natalia was right. It was a fight between Marcus and P. John.

Mrs. Hocker had offered Dinky a piece of chocolate-fudge cake which Marcus' mother had made, and P. John had ordered Dinky to refuse it.

Marcus had taken it as a personal insult.

Marcus had started screaming at P. John, "If she doesn't taste my mother's cake, I'll split, man, and take your left ear with me!"

By this time Tucker and Natalia had run down the hall and were watching the scene near the entrance to the living room.

"You *try* taking my left anything!" P. John answered, standing up to face Marcus, and P. John had a point, because Marcus didn't even come up to P. John's shoulder.

"Just *taste* the cake, honey, just a taste," Mrs. Hocker said.

"Let's all cool off, now," Mr. Hocker said.

"Susan doesn't eat chocolate anymore," P. John said.

"That's *my mother's* chocolate!" Marcus said, crouching like a jungle cat about to spring.

"Dinky," Mrs. Hocker said, "it's only polite."

"I don't eat chocolate anymore," Dinky said.

"She'll have a taste later," Mr. Hocker said.

"She will not!" P. John said, and then Marcus sprang, catching hold of P. John's neck, and trying to pummel P. John's stomach with his fists.

P. John caught Marcus' arms and twisted them around behind his back, while Marcus winced with pain.

Then Marcus began to cry, and P. John let him go.

"Get out of our house," Mrs. Hocker said to P. John. "Get out right now."

"This can all be settled peacefully," Mr. Hocker began.

But Mrs. Hocker was way out of control. "Get out! Don't you *ever* come back! Out! Now!"

Dinky began to cry, too.

Mrs. Hocker had her arms around Marcus. Mr. Hocker was standing in front of Dinky, offering her his handkerchief and saying, "Here, here, now."

Everyone else was just milling around helplessly, except P. John, who had gone back to the bedroom for his coat. He stormed past Tucker and Natalia without seeing them.

The front door slammed.

SEVEN

THREE DAYS before Christmas, P. John Knight got up in Creative Writing and read his new short story, "Answered Prayers."

It was science fiction.

It was about a future world entirely under the control of one man and one woman: Mama and Papa. Everyone took dope which Mama and Papa gave them. Everyone had the same last name: Love. The people with high I.Q.'s became slaves, and took care of the machines which did all the work. Everyone else sat around in stupors, listening to television sets saying, "Mama loves you. Papa loves you," and watching the word "Love" spelled out in endless animated designs.

There were no wars and no one went hungry. Everyone lived like everyone else, regardless of race or color, except for "the brains," who lived in automated prisons guarded by automatons.

"Any comments from the class?" Mr. Baird, the writing instructor, said when P. John was finished.

"What does the title mean?" someone asked.

"There's an old saying," P. John said. "When God wants to punish you, he answers your prayers. In this world everyone's prayers are finally answered."

Someone else said, "What about 'the brains'? Their prayers aren't answered."

P. John said, "Oh, 'the brains' never prayed in the first place. They didn't believe in God."

"But no one has a good deal in your world," another student said.

"Mama and Papa do," P. John said.

"What does it all mean?" a girl asked.

P. John shrugged. "It means what it says. It's a story of the future. It's a story of what will happen to the world after everyone's on dope and welfare."

Someone booed, and someone else called out, "Bigot!"

It was almost time for the last bell.

Mr. Baird hopped up on his desk, and sat with his legs crossed in front of him. "P. John," he said. "Let me try and speak for the class. I'm picking up their vibes loud and clear."

"No one else in this class even finishes an assignment but me," P. John said. That was almost true. P. John regularly completed every assignment. The students liked to say of P. John that he lived a life of E's, because P. John never received any other mark, no matter the course.

"That's not the point under discussion," Mr. Baird said. "We're discussing your latest work, P. John, and while your imagination blows our minds, your philosophy is often a downer. . . . P. John, you don't feel for people."

"I don't feel for junkies, that's true," P. John said. "I don't believe in mollycoddling people, that's true."

"Hasn't your own head ever been messed up?" Mr. Baird asked.

"His head is messed up right now!" someone shouted out.

"When I have problems, I have to solve them myself," P. John said.

"Fine," Mr. Baird said. "But what about people who don't have your same opportunity in life, or your strength?"

"You're not discussing my story," P. John said. "You're lecturing me."

The bell rang.

Mr. Baird threw up his hands. "Okay," he said. "There's no more time. . . . P. John, you could use more compassion. You really could. . . . As for the rest of you, enjoy your vacation and Merry Christmas."

Tucker waited for P. John outside the classroom. They walked to their lockers together.

Tucker said, "That was a neat story, but what did it mean?"

"It's fantasy," P. John said. "You shouldn't analyze fantasy too much. You're supposed to feel it;

you're not supposed to intellectualize it."

"Parents don't come off too well in it," Tucker said.

"Maybe they're not parents," P. John said. "Maybe Mama and Papa are just society, or the state, or the Mafia. Don't understand me too quickly. A famous philosopher said that." Then P. John changed the subject. "Any more news from Susan?"

"Didn't you see her last night?"

"She didn't show up at Weight Watchers. I tried to call her, but I got Mr. Hocker. He said she was at church. I'm supposed to believe *that*."

"She *was* at church," Tucker said. "The Heights Church is holding a five-day bazaar. All the merchants and organizations in the Heights have booths set up in the church house. Dinky's working in the DRI booth."

"What's that?"

"Drug Rehabilitation, Inc.," Tucker said. "DRI, for short. It's her mother's organization."

"Hasn't she sent me a message?" P. John asked.

"Not since the day before yesterday."

Help Yourself had a booth at the bazaar, too, and Tucker had been helping out. Dinky had sent P. John a message telling him she'd see him at Weight Watchers. What had happened between then and now, Tucker didn't know.

"I've got a Christmas present for her," P. John said. "How'm I going to get it to her?"

"I could pick it up now, I suppose," Tucker said.

"I guess it's the only way," P. John said. "Would you mind, Tucker?"

Richter School was a private school, and most of the students came from what some people called "good families." That was supposed to imply that the families were what Tucker's mother liked to describe as "comfortable." The fathers were in professions like law, medicine, public relations, banking, advertising, publishing.

Most of the students lived in large apartment houses with doormen, and some lived in town houses like Tucker did.

P. John lived on the third floor of a rickety old building on West 13th Street, no doorman and no elevator. It was Tucker's first visit there.

"My mother's dead," P. John said out of the blue as they climbed the worn stairs. "There's just my father and me."

The first thing Tucker saw when P. John opened the door to his apartment was a huge poster of Mao Tse-tung on the kitchen wall, and beside that, a poster reading BEAT THE SYSTEM!

There was a lean, boyish-faced man at the stove. He was stirring a large pot of spaghetti sauce. He had an apron around his waist; he was wearing worn khaki pants, desert boots, and a white T-shirt with a picture of Bach on the front. He had long salt-and-pepper hair, and a wide, friendly grin.

"Welcome!" he said, "I'm Perry. Who're you?"

"This is Tucker Woolf, a classmate," P. John said. "He came by to pick up something."

"Stay to dinner, Tucker," said Mr. Knight. "P. John, I've invited Mac to dinner, and Dewey. Dewey's here from the Coast."

"Thank you, anyway," Tucker said. "I'm expected home."

"Only four for dinner," Mr. Knight said. "That's a pity. I'm cooking enough for an army. I'm adding to what we had last night, Johnny."

"Only *three* for dinner," P. John said. "I'm not going off my diet again."

"No one's twisting your arm, Johnny. I really admire you, turning down your favorite dish."

P. John said nothing. He led Tucker into the next room. All four walls were bookcases. There was a card table filled with magazines and notebooks, and a large steel file cabinet beside it.

"My father's writing a book," P. John muttered. He went across to a claw-legged bureau and picked up a gift-wrapped parcel that was obviously a book.

There was an old couch with a worn throw across it, a threadbare rug on the floor, a few captain's chairs, and a long coffee table made from a piece of slate and some bricks.

"Do you want to sit down?" P. John said.

"Maybe I just better go along," Tucker said.

"Sit down and stay awhile," P. John's father called from the kitchen. "Johnny never brings friends here. He's ashamed of me."

"I'm not ashamed of you," P. John called back. "I just don't agree with most of your opinions."

P. John handed Tucker the gift-wrapped book. "Tell her there's a card inside."

"What's Johnny's girl friend like?" P. John's father called in. "He won't tell me a thing."

"She's very nice," Tucker shouted, but Mr. Knight appeared in the doorway, wiping his hands on his apron, lighting up a cigarette.

"Why don't you call home and see if you can stay for dinner?" Mr. Knight said. "You'll like these two old friends of mine. They've seen some hard times. They have a lot of interesting stories to tell."

"All adding up to one thing," P. John said. "They're out of work, and they want to borrow money."

"I really have to go home. Thanks anyway," Tucker said.

"Dewey just got a job in a department store," Mr. Knight said. "But *if* Mac and Dewey wanted to borrow money, we'd lend them money. They're our friends, Johnny."

"They're your friends. I don't make loans."

"Johnny thinks I'm a soft touch," Mr. Knight said to Tucker.

"I don't think it. I know it," P. John said. "It's open house for the takers around here. Give us your tired, your poor, your huddled masses, and we'll feed them and put them on the dole."

Everyone was still standing.

Mr. Knight said, "Johnny's still sore at me. We'd saved some money to buy him a good watch, and I spent it."

"He *gave* it to some migrant workers," P. John said. "Another of his donations."

"You blew a wad on Weight Watchers, Johnny," Mr. Knight said. "You could have bought a couple of watches with that."

They seemed to forget Tucker was in the room.

"I earned every cent of it myself, working in Brentano's," P. John said.

"And I admire you, Johnny, but you're still better off than a migrant worker."

"Sometimes I wonder."

"You go to a private school. You have a nice, respectable job after school in a bookstore. You can buy a little Christmas gift for your girl," Mr. Knight said. "I don't sing any sad songs for you, Johnny."

"You sing them all for tramps and beggars and migrant workers," P. John said. "Don't I know *that!*"

Tucker managed to think of something to say finally. "What's your book about, Mr. Knight?" he said.

"It's called *Reason and Responsibility*," Mr. Knight answered. "It's about sharing privilege."

"It's about handouts," P. John said.

The noise of the spaghetti boiling over in the kitchen interrupted the conversation. Mr. Knight ran in to attend to it.

"I like him," Tucker told P. John.

"I don't *dislike* him," P. John answered.

"This is going to be delicious spaghetti, Johnny," Mr. Knight called from the other room. "Even better than last night."

"He really likes it that I'm fat," P. John said.

"It's the only way he can feel superior to me."

Tucker didn't know what to answer. He said, "I never knew you worked in a bookstore."

"Tell her to try and call me," P. John said, ending the conversation and leading Tucker toward the door. "Every time I call her they say she's out."

EIGHT

HELP YOURSELF TO CHRISTMAS
Help Yourself: Opening December 26th on
Montague Street!
* *Give a basket of Natural Foods.*
* *Give a Juicer, a Sprouter, a Yogurt Maker.*
* *Give healthy fruit & nut mixes.*
* *Give a darn about your/her/his/their health*
  this CHRISTMAS!

TUCKER'S MOTHER was tending the booth at the church bazaar.

"Where've you been?" she said. "It's almost six o'clock."

"I stopped by at this guy's apartment."

"P. John Knight's apartment?" his mother said.

"Yeah."

"Tucker, I want to talk to you about him."

"What about him?"

"Not here. Jingle's going to relieve me at six," she said. "Do you want to have dinner with me at the deli?"

"Sure," Tucker said. "I'd like to see Dinky Hocker first. Is she here?"

"She's here," Mrs. Woolf said, "but I think we'd better have a talk before you see her."

Jingle arrived in a large fur hat, smiling, reeking of martinis. He said to Tucker's mother, "Cal went into New York today to see about that job, didn't he?"

"How much gin did it take to give you the courage to ask that question?" she said.

"I don't need him, anyway," Jingle answered. "I'll run the store myself. *My* way."

"Just don't smoke too many cigarettes while you mind the booth," she said. "It doesn't look good."

"Tucker and I don't care how things look, do we Tucker?" Jingle said. He shoved his elbow into Tucker's side and winked. "You take after your uncle, don't you, Tucker? We don't care how things look. Let 'em talk," and he laughed as though he and Tucker shared a private joke.

At the deli, Tucker asked his mother, "What did Jingle mean?"

"I'm going to get to that, Tucker," she said.

"Jingle overheard a conversation I had this afternoon with Mrs. Hocker."

"Didn't you go to work today?"

"I took the day off to help at the bazaar. Your father went to see about that fund-raising job."

"I thought he was never happy being a fund-raiser?"

"You know better than that. So do I. But your father's been going through a lot since he was fired. He was hurt by that."

"What did Mrs. Hocker say?" Tucker asked.

"I'm getting to that, Tucker. I want you to understand why your father and I haven't been paying much attention to you lately."

"I get it," Tucker said.

"Do you really? Because I know you've been going through a lot, too."

"Is that what Mrs. Hocker said?"

"Mrs. Hocker said you've been trying to be very attentive to her niece."

"I haven't been *trying*," Tucker said. "I'm not even sure I've been that attentive."

"Are you falling for Natalia, Tucker?"

"Falling for her?"

"Tucker, don't pretend I'm talking Latin to you. You know exactly what I mean!"

"What difference does it make?" Tucker said. "Do we have to settle it right now, over hamburgers?"

"Tucker, Mrs. Hocker thinks you're a little too involved with the girl."

"So what?"

"You know the girl's background."

"Some of it. She's been in a special school," Tucker said.

"She's from a very, very, bad background," his mother said. "It wasn't easy for Helen Hocker to tell me about it. It's her sister's child, you know."

"I'm not planning to marry her yet."

"Tucker, don't be flip! Natalia Line isn't your ordinary high-school girl. Her mother was a mental case, and her father killed himself."

"Oh." Tucker let that information digest.

"Yes. She's been through a great deal in her fifteen years."

Tucker took a bite of his hamburger. He finally said, "Well, what's that got to do with what we do together?"

"What *do* you do together?"

"Nothing," Tucker said. "Nothing special."

"Mrs. Hocker said she never hears any talking when she goes by a room with you and Natalia in it."

"We're not great talkers."

"What do you do together?" his mother said, "What kind of a relationship is it?"

"We listen to records and stuff."

"Sitting on the same bed in the bedroom?"

"Yeah."

"Tucker, Mrs. Hocker doesn't want you closing yourself off in a bedroom with Natalia."

"The door's always open. That's where the record player is. That's where Nader usually is."

"Don't do it anymore."

"Okay."

"Mrs. Hocker thinks her niece isn't ready for such an emotional involvement."

"Okay, I'll ignore her," Tucker said.

"Don't ignore her. In fact, you've been invited for Christmas supper," his mother said. "But don't lock yourself away with the girl."

"For Pete's sake!" Tucker said.

"And there's something else."

"What?"

"This P. John Knight. *I* didn't particularly like him. Your father didn't like him at all. And Mr. and Mrs. Hocker don't want Dinky to see him again. He's very hostile."

"He's really not a bad guy," Tucker said.

"I heard about that Friday night," his mother said. "Mrs. Hocker works very hard for DRI. She really cares about those young people. She's a very earnest woman, Tucker. This world could use more people like her, people who care what happens to the less fortunate."

"Look at it from Dinky's viewpoint," Tucker said. "She's never had a boyfriend, Mom."

"That's the point."

"What's the point?"

"She's gone overboard for this Knight boy. He's a bad influence. All the things the Hockers believe in, he belittles."

"Mom, P. John means well. He wants to help Dinky lose weight."

"The Hockers would rather have her plump and

unprejudiced than thin and intolerant," Mrs. Woolf said.

"I bet that's something Mrs. Hocker said."

"Nevertheless," his mother admitted, "don't you do anything to encourage the relationship."

"Relationship," Tucker sighed unhappily. "They've only had one real date."

"And one real date isn't enough to warrant a forty-dollar gold watch, is it?"

"What're you talking about?" Tucker said.

"Dinky went out and spent forty dollars on him for Christmas," his mother said. "She bought him a watch."

"She did?"

"She did. Mrs. Hocker is returning it."

"Where'd she get forty dollars?"

"That's not the point, Tucker."

"I get the point," Tucker said.

"Are you sure?"

"I get it," Tucker said, "but I think Mrs. Hocker is wrong about everything."

"That's not for you to decide."

Tucker shrugged. He didn't say anything about the gift for Dinky from P. John, which he was still carrying in his book bag.

His mother wasn't quite finished. "About going over there for Christmas supper," she said. "No one is going to exchange gifts, so don't buy anything for Natalia. The Hockers have already bought the girls' presents."

"Am I just going to go over there empty-handed?"

"Take Mrs. Hocker a plant. I'll give you the money."

"And a Merry Christmas to all," Tucker said.

"Honey," his mother said, "try to understand. Mrs. Hocker is a *good* woman. She's trying to do what she thinks is best for both girls."

Then she shook her head regretfully. "Your father and I shouldn't have teased you about being in love. We didn't know the circumstances."

"What *are* the circumstances?" Tucker complained. "Natalia and I are just friends!"

"I'm going to take your word for that, Tucker."

"Oh, thanks a lot," Tucker said sarcastically.

When they were finished eating, Tucker walked his mother back to the bazaar. For a while he hung around hoping he would see Dinky. Then he saw the Hockers, who told him Dinky was home. They were both on duty at the DRI booth, with Marcus helping, too. There was a huge poster in front of the booth listing all the terms for dope, from "snow" to "smack." By the time Mrs. Hocker was off working for another needy cause, everyone in Brooklyn Heights would know junky jargon as well as he knew the alphabet.

When Tucker arrived back at the town house, he sat down in front of the telephone. Then he paced around the room for a while, and finally he dialed.

Natalia answered.

"I hear I'll see you Christmas day," he said.

He was almost sure she'd rhyme it with "Hooray," or "You may," but instead she said, "I'm making you a little gift."

"I'm making you one, too," he said, which was a lie, but not a lie he couldn't make into a truth. No one had said he couldn't present her with something homemade, only that he couldn't *buy* her a gift.

"We both had the same idea," she said.

"Yeah, we did," he said.

"I'm alone here," she said. "Just Nader and me. Do you want to come over for a while?"

"I better not," he said.

"Can't you?" she sounded disappointed.

"I've had a rough day," he said.

"Why has it been rough?"

He felt foolish telling her anything had been rough for him, after what his mother said Natalia'd been through in fifteen years. He said, "It hasn't really been that rough. What have you been doing?

"After school I read this book: *The Little Prince.*"

"I've heard of that book," he said. He didn't tell her about seeing the excerpt from the book on the sermon board that day, and then rushing to the Hockers' to bawl out Dinky over feeding Nader too much.

The Little Prince had been responsible, in a way, for their meeting.

After the talk with his mother, Tucker felt self-conscious about their "relationship." He didn't know, himself, what kind of a relationship it was.

"It's a beautiful book, Tucker," she said.

He realized they were actually having a conversation. It was a lucky thing, too, because their chances of ever going off to play the Balloon Game quietly together were nil from now on.

"I'll get a copy and read it," he said.

"Really?"

"Sure," he said.

"It's starting to snow again."

"It'll be a White Christmas," he said.

"I'm glad you're coming over."

"I am, too."

"Well, I'll see you then," she said.

"Yeah. Great."

"Great," she said. "Good night, Tucker."

For a long while after Tucker hung up, he just sat there. He realized he still had on his coat, but it didn't matter. He felt very comfortable, and very happy.

It didn't occur to him to wonder why Natalia was over there alone . . . or where Dinky was.

NINE

WHEN TUCKER woke up the next morning, his mother was already at work. His father was sitting at the kitchen table sipping papaya-mint tea.

"Would it bother you if I made scrambled eggs and bacon for myself?" Tucker asked.

"No, go ahead," his father said. "I already had groats."

"Don't you miss the old food at all?" Tucker asked, getting a carton of eggs from the refrigerator.

"That isn't all I miss," his father said. He pointed to a manuscript his mother had left on the kitchen table. "I miss the days when your mother didn't have to waste her good mind doing that sort of work."

The manuscript was called, "I Left My Husband for a Jesus Freak."

"Hey," Tucker said. "Mom was working on that last night. That's a rush job for the April issue."

"She forgot it this morning," his father said. "Would you mind taking it into New York, Tucker?"

"No. I'll take it in right after breakfast."

"Tucker," his father said, "how are you? I feel as though I've lost touch with you, too."

"I'm okay, Dad."

"Maybe this health-store thing was a bad idea," Tucker's father said.

"Why don't you just let Jingle run it?"

"I can't do that, Tucker. If Jingle had his way he'd mark up everything way beyond cost. He'd claim things were organically grown that weren't organically grown. I don't want our name on a crooked health store."

"Then what are you going to do?" Tucker said.

"I'm going to go through with what I started," his father said. "I'm going to run it as well as I know how. I'm going to personally sample everything I sell, too."

Tucker groaned.

"I didn't say you and your mother had to sample all of it," his father said.

"She'll go along with it, though," Tucker said.

"Yes, she probably will," his father agreed. "She's a great woman. I don't know how she ever got a brother like Jingle."

"Who won the argument over the sleigh bed?" Tucker asked.

His father said, "I told Jingle that thing has to

99

be out of there no later than Christmas Day."

The telephone rang then, and Tucker's father went into the living room to answer it. Tucker put some bacon in the frying pan, and glanced down at his mother's manuscript while he waited for the bacon to cook. The story had been written by a woman from a small town in Texas. The opening sentences read:

> *He had a lopsided grin and round brown eyes, with golden hair below his shoulders and tight ragged jeans clinging to his long, strong legs. He was telling me about Jesus in a low, purring voice, and for a slow second while my heart beat like a tom-tom, I forgot I was a married woman with a baby on the way.*

Tucker's father reappeared in the kitchen and said, "It's your friend the Nazi on the phone. I told him you were making breakfast, but he says it's urgent."

"Watch my bacon, okay?" Tucker said.

When Tucker said "Hello," P. John said, "I have to see you right away, Tucker. There's been a lot of trouble, thanks to the Hockers."

"What kind of trouble?"

"Trouble with the police and everything," P. John said. "I can't go into it. I'm at work. Can you meet me during my lunch break?"

Tucker agreed to meet him outside Brentano's bookstore in Greenwich Village at noon.

He went back to the kitchen. His father was busy at the stove.

"Tucker, do you want fried or scrambled?"

"Scrambled, thanks."

"Tucker," his father said, "I'm not going to dictate to you what kind of friends to pal around with. But that particular fellow has problems, if you want my opinion."

"Who doesn't?" Tucker said. .

"That's right, who doesn't," his father said. "But you have to choose between people with sympathetic problems, and people with unsympathetic problems. How can you sympathize with someone whose problem seems to be that he thinks he's superior to the underdog?"

"Don't understand him too quickly," Tucker said.

"Well don't *you* waste too much time understanding him, either."

"I won't" Tucker said. "Hey, I can't eat six eggs, Dad!"

"Then I'll have to help you," his father said.

Tucker left the manuscript with the receptionist at *Stirring Romances*, and then took the subway to the Village.

When he reached Brentano's, he saw P. John already out front waiting for him. P. John was eating a hot dog.

"I thought we were going to eat something together," Tucker said.

"We are. I'm just warming up to it."

"What happened to Weight Watchers?"

"I'm too nervous to eat legal food today," P. John said. "C'mon, we'll go down the street to Nathan's. I can eat ten more of these."

"What happened?" Tucker said.

While they stood at the counter in Nathan's, waiting for their food, P. John told him.

Dinky had appeared suddenly at the Knights' apartment last night while they were all having supper. Mr. Knight had invited her to stay. Dinky, P. John, Mr. Knight, Mac, and Dewey were sitting around the table in the kitchen, after an immense spaghetti dinner, when the police arrived.

At the Hockers' request, the police were looking for Dinky, but when they saw the posters of Mao, and the BEAT THE SYSTEM posters, they began questioning everyone. The man named Dewey was a Mexican who had entered the country illegally.

"He isn't supposed to be working here, either," P. John said. "When the police found out he had a job, they arrested him."

"Why did he tell them he had a job?"

"They knew by looking at him," P. John said. "He'd just come from work. He's been working as a Santa Claus in a department store."

The police took Dewey away, and the Hockers were called to pick up Dinky.

"That's bad," Tucker sympathized. "What did the Hockers have to say when they got there?"

"They fell all over my father when they found out who he was."

"Who is he?" Tucker said.

"Perry Knight. It wouldn't mean anything to you. But they knew his books. Some people think he's this great thinker," P. John said. "That's why I never call myself Perry. I don't want people identifying me with him."

"So the Hockers weren't mad?" Tucker asked.

"Wrong! They felt really bad because Dewey was arrested. Dewey is this big liberal, too. He works with those migrant workers. My father's friends are all involved in politics. They're always hanging around our place sponging off us."

"Well, tell me what happened!" Tucker said.

"The Hockers heard me fighting with my father. They heard me say I was glad Dewey was arrested. I was, too. I am! I'm tired of Mac and Dewey and all of them!" P. John said emphatically. "My father cares more about what happens to them than he cares about me! The only reason I can afford to go to a school like Richter is that my mother's insurance money was left to me! My father would have given that money away!"

"Go on," Tucker said.

P. John shrugged. "They took Susan back to the Heights. They told my father they'd prefer me to stay out of her life. You know what he said?"

"What?"

"He said he knew what they meant, that I had a lot to learn. . . . Susan was crying. She said she'd saved up all the money she used to spend on snacks to buy me a gold watch. She said her mother returned it."

"That's where she got the money. You mean she was spending that much money a week on food?"

"A week. Ten days. Sure. It isn't inexpensive to be fat, you know."

P. John poured the mustard over four hot dogs and passed it to Tucker.

He said, "And then my father made this little speech. He said the trouble was, we were both fat cats. He said we were overweight and overprivileged. He said whole families lived for months on what that gold watch had cost Susan. He said two young people who had to put good money into an organization that kept them from making pigs of themselves were two very self-indulgent teenagers. He was furious, you know, because of Dewey's arrest, and he just let fly."

"Is Dewey going to stay in jail?" Tucker said.

"Mr. Hocker's going to try and help him," P. John said. "But he'll probably be deported again. I don't care what happens to him. I'm going away."

"Where?"

"I have an aunt in Maine. I'm going to go there. I'll probably stay there."

"Are you going to tell your father?"

"He suggested it," P. John said.

"Gee, I'm sorry, P. John."

"I'm not," P. John said. "She's my mother's sister. . . . Make sure Susan gets my Christmas present, okay?"

"Sure." Then Tucker said. "I'll miss you, P."

"My mother was a Republican," P. John said.

"I don't know what she saw in *him*. . . . Love is blind, all right."

"Susan will miss you, too."

"Thanks for finally calling her Susan," P. John said. "Do me a favor and always call her that from now on."

P. John went back to Brentano's, and for a while Tucker wandered around the Village looking for last-minute stocking gifts for his mother. Every year he and his father made a stocking for her from "Santa Claus." Tucker had promised to pick up a few things for it.

His heart wasn't in it at all. He kept thinking over what P. John had said, trying to sympathize with the things Mr. Knight had told the Hockers. All of it was true, Tucker knew, but there was P. John working during his Christmas vacation, and Tucker was just hanging loose; and there was P. John being called a fat cat, and Mr. Knight cooking up pots of spaghetti.

Tucker felt more and more down, and even worse when he spotted this old man with bloodshot eyes standing on the corner of Eighth Street and Sixth Avenue.

He was unshaven and dressed in an overcoat several sizes larger than he was. His breath smelled like Jingle's after five o'clock in the afternoon. He was giving away red and green balloons, and croaking out "Merry Christmas from Shipp's" to anyone who would take one.

Written on every balloon were these words:

CHRITMA I$ FOR GIFT$

LOAN$ ARE EA$Y AT
$HIPP $AVING$ CO.

TEN

"MERRY CHRISTMAS, Natalia. Merry Christmas, Susan. Merry Christmas, Nader. Merry Christmas, Mr. and Mrs. Hocker. . . . Merry Christmas, Marcus."

"Merry Christmas, Tucker," Mrs. Hocker said. "Put your coat back in Dinky's room."

"This is for you," Tucker said, handing Mrs. Hocker the poinsettia plant.

"Isn't this beautiful! Look at this, Horace."

"Beautiful," Mr. Hocker said.

"Oh, Tucker?" Mrs. Hocker said as he started down the hall.

"Yes?"

"Leave your book bag up here."

Tucker had three gifts in the book bag: the two he had made for Dinky and Natalia, and P. John's gift to Dinky.

Tucker shifted his weight from one foot to the other, and stood there a moment with the book bag under his arm. He said, "There's not much in it, Mrs. Hocker."

"We've all had our Christmas," she said, "and we had a rule that we wouldn't exchange gifts. But I realize Natalia made something for you, and you made something for her. It's all right, Tucker. Leave the book bag up here. We're all curious to see your homemade gifts."

Tucker came back reluctantly and set the book bag down in the hall.

Then he went to the back of the house and removed his coat, put it on Dinky's bed, and sat down to take off his boots.

Marcus appeared in the doorway. "You want a glass of champagne, man? I'm bartender."

"I don't drink," Tucker said.

"I know that, man, but everyone has one glass of champagne today."

"Okay," Tucker said.

"That cat of yours has been acting crazy," Marcus said. "That cat's been tearing around ripping up the place."

"It's Susan's cat," Tucker said.

"She's been acting crazy, too. What's going on, man? What's she in the doghouse about?"

"I don't know," Tucker shrugged.

"How come you're calling her Susan now?"

"Because that's her name."

"What's the matter, man? Don't you want to be friends?"

"Sure, Marcus," Tucker said. "I'm just down." Tucker wondered if he could pretend P. John's gift was something he'd bought for Dinky himself before his mother told him gifts weren't being exchanged. Then he remembered P. John said there was a note from him inside. No way.

"I used to feel that down a long time ago," Marcus said. "I'd take my pillow out and look for trouble, you know what I mean?"

"Your pillow?" Tucker said.

"I used to take a pillow with me in the summer. Pretend I was going up on a roof for some sun, you know? Then I'd use the pillow to muffle the sound of the glass when I broke a window. I'd look around the pad fast and grab what I could and *pow!*—back down the fire escape with a radio, a camera, anything I could pass to a fence. Then I'd shoot some smack and nod off, man."

"I get it," Tucker said.

"But don't get me wrong, my head was messed up then."

The living room was trimmed with holly and pine branches, and there was a tall tree with blue lights, blue bulbs and silver tinsel. Mrs. Hocker was playing the piano and singing, "Hark! what mean those holy voices,/Sweetly sounding through the skies?" Mr. Hocker was sitting beside her on the piano bench, sipping champagne. Dinky was pulling Nader away from the poinsettia plant on the coffee table. Natalia was on the couch, and when Tucker walked in, she patted the cushion next to her and smiled.

Tucker walked across and sat down. "Hi," he said.

"Hi. Merry Christmas."

"Merry Christmas," he said, and then he looked under the tree. There in a row were the three gifts he had carried over in his book bag.

" 'Lo! the angelic host rejoices,' " Mrs. Hocker sang. " 'Heavenly alleluias rise.' "

Marcus appeared with a glass of champagne for Tucker.

"Nurse it along, man. Only one apiece," he said.

Mrs. Hocker stopped playing the piano. She said, "Tucker? Would you like to give Natalia her gifts now? I know she'd like to give you yours."

Tucker looked at Natalia. "You go first," he said.

"I only made you one," she said softly.

"That's all I made you," he said.

"But there's three gifts there."

"I only made you one," he repeated.

Natalia went across to the tree, reached behind it, and walked back, handing Tucker a small package wrapped in Noël paper.

"Christmas gifts should never be secret," Mrs. Hocker said. "We should share our joy at Christmas."

Natalia blushed.

"Joy, joy, joy," Dinky recited in a bored voice.

"Open your gift, Tucker," Mr. Hocker said.

Tucker tore off the wrapping. Natalia had made him a tiny doll wearing a gold paper crown and a royal blue paper robe, with cotton dotting it like small patches of white fur.

"It's the prince," Natalia said.

"The Prince of Peace," Mrs. Hocker said. "How nice, Natalia!"

"It's the Little Prince," Natalia said to Tucker.

There was very tiny printing across the gold crown. No one seemed to notice that but Tucker.

"What a lovely gift, isn't it a lovely gift, Tucker?" Mrs. Hocker said.

"Yes," Tucker said. He could barely make out the words: *If you tame me, then we shall need each other.*

Tucker was amazed. She had not only selected the very book which was responsible for their meeting, but the very words from that book, too.

"A lovely gift, a lovely thought," Mrs. Hocker continued. "Dinky, if Nader eats that plant, we're just going to have to have a talk about Nader's future."

"Nader and I don't have a future," Dinky said.

Marcus laughed appreciatively.

"Put some pepper in the plant," Mr. Hocker said. "That'll keep Nader away."

"What a good idea!" Mrs. Hocker said.

Tucker turned to Natalia and whispered, "There's an amazing coincidence I'll tell you about. Remind me to tell you."

"What are you whispering to Natalia?" Mrs. Hocker said, trying to sound light and merry, but sounding heavy and snoopy, instead.

"He's probably discussing their relationship," Dinky said.

Marcus laughed again.

Mrs. Hocker said, "Dinky, I know you *think* you're amusing, but don't test my patience too much, sweetheart."

Mr. Hocker had gone to the kitchen, and returned with the pepper mill.

He began grinding pepper over the poinsettia plant.

"Now it's your turn, Tucker," Mrs. Hocker said.

Tucker said, "I made something for Susan *and* Natalia."

"Oh my my my my my," Mrs. Hocker said. "How formal we are. Susan. All right. Let's see *Susan's* gift first."

As Tucker went across to the tree for it, Mrs. Hocker said to Marcus, "After Dinky opens her gift, Marcus, you fetch her another glass of water."

"She's drinking a lot of water, isn't she?" Mr. Hocker said.

"It's her own idea," Mrs. Hocker said. "She wants to try a new diet. The Stillman Quick-Weight-Loss Diet. She has to drink eight ten-ounce glasses of water a day. I'm trying to help her remember."

Tucker handed Dinky her gift. His mother had wrapped it, and tied it with a red bow. It was a small piece of black cardboard with white lettering and a yellow border. Tucker had shellacked it to make it look like a plaque.

Dinky unwrapped it and looked at it, frowning.

"It's a line from a short story by Kurt Vonnegut, Jr.," Tucker explained. "A story in *Welcome to the Monkey House*."

"What does it say?" Mrs. Hocker asked.

Dinky read it. " 'You are better than you think. A-one, a-two, a-three.' "

"The director of this high-school band used to tell the kids that, every time he raised his baton," Tucker said.

"Do you want your water now, Dinky?" Marcus said.

"Yes, get her the water," Mrs. Hocker said.

For a moment, Dinky looked as though she were going to cry. She was probably thinking of P. John, remembering how P. John had said you'd never find Kurt Vonnegut, Jr., on welfare.

Tucker had gone to the library and searched through Vonnegut for a quote. He hadn't done it to make Dinky sad, but to tell Dinky that P. John was there for Christmas, anyway, despite her mother and father. His presence was in the room.

" 'You are better than you think. A-one, a-two, a-three,' " Dinky repeated, and then she let out this great guffaw.

"It's a strange sentiment for Christmas," Mrs. Hocker said. "We shouldn't be thinking how much better we are, but how blessed we are."

"It's a valid sentiment," Mr. Hocker said. "We

always tell our DRI members that they have to love themselves before they can love others."

"Right on!" Marcus said, appearing with a ten-ounce glass of water for Dinky.

"I don't think Dinky has any problem loving herself," Mrs. Hocker said.

"Here's mud in your eye!" Dinky held the water up in a toast to her mother, and drank it down chug-a-lug.

"At Renaissance we had this saying of Eleanor Roosevelt's on our bulletin board," Natalia said. " 'No one can make you feel inferior without your consent.' "

Marcus said, "What's Renaissance?"

"We're not going into that now," Mrs. Hocker said.

"I don't mind answering," Natalia said.

"Natalia. *Dear.*" Mrs. Hocker said. "We don't wash our dirty linen in public."

"That's not a good way to put it," Mr. Hocker said.

Mrs. Hocker stood up and put her finger to her lips. "Hush, hush, hush, *everyone!* What is all this silly talk about feeling inferior, and being better than you think you are? We're not conducting a therapy session, after all. This is Christmas!"

"I'm sorry if I started something," Tucker said.

"I'm not sorry," Dinky said.

"Dinky. *Sweetheart.* Thank Tucker for your gift and let's continue. The Heights Carollers will be calling soon."

"Thanks, Tucker."

"You're welcome, Susan."

"Now, Tucker, give Natalia her two gifts," Mrs. Hocker said.

Tucker didn't know what to do then, so he went over to the tree and got Natalia's gift, leaving behind P. John's gift to Dinky.

Tucker's gift had been inspired by two things: The Balloon Game he played with Natalia, and the man he had seen in the Village giving away the balloons advertising the loan company. Tucker had bought seven balloons, one for every day of the week. He had written the beginning of a sentence on each one, with dashes after the words, for Natalia to fill in her own sentiments.

It didn't look like much of anything when Natalia unwrapped the paper. Seven, limp, deflated balloons.

"What *is* that?" Mrs. Hocker said.

"You have to blow each one up," Tucker told Natalia.

Natalia picked out a blue one and blew it up.

It said, "I care—"

Natalia smiled. "I care about people who care about me."

"You see," Tucker said to Mrs. Hocker, "you fill in the sentence whatever way you want to."

Mrs. Hocker said, "You do?"

"I care about very little in life," Dinky said.

"I care about having something to eat soon," Mr. Hocker chuckled.

Mrs. Hocker was frowning. "You have a strange turn of mind, Tucker."

"It's an inside joke," Dinky said. "You just don't get it."

"It's not an inside joke," Tucker protested.

"I care about staying straight," Marcus said. "Oh man, I don't care about anything but keeping my head straight."

"Horace," Mrs. Hocker said, "everything is set up for the buffet. Carry the dishes into the dining room, and the girls can serve everyone."

"There's one gift left under the tree," Mr. Hocker said.

Tucker didn't see any way out. He said quietly, "That's for Susan."

"Another gift for our Dinky?" Mrs. Hocker questioned him.

Tucker felt his face get warm. "Yes," he said. He went over and took P. John's gift from under the tree, and handed it to Dinky.

"It's not exactly from me," he said.

"What does that mean?" Mrs. Hocker said.

"It's not from me."

"I know who it's from," Dinky said. She held it as though someone were about to pry it away from her.

Mrs. Hocker just sat there with this tight little smile. "Very well, Dinky. Open it."

"I don't want to open it here."

"*Open* it, sweetheart. It's perfectly all right."

"It's a book, that's all," Dinky said. "I'll open it later."

"Dinky, we all know it's a gift from your friend P. John Knight. Now, open it. Your father's hungry, and the Carollers will be by soon."

Dinky took her time pulling the ribbon and carefully undoing the Scotch tape at both ends. Then she slid the book out from its wrapping.

It was a copy of *Weight Watchers Cook Book* by Jean Nidetch.

"Oh my my my my my. Isn't *that* romantic," Mrs. Hocker remarked sarcastically.

"Helen," Mr. Hocker said softly, "don't."

Marcus began blowing up the six other balloons for Natalia.

Dinky still sat there looking at the book, saying nothing. Her head was bent, so Tucker could not see the expression on her face.

"I'll get the food ready," Mr. Hocker said.

"I think I see a card peeking out from the pages," Mrs. Hocker said. For some reason, Mrs. Hocker seemed peculiarly pleased.

Dinky became resigned to what her mother was going to make her do. Mechanically, she took out the card. It was enclosed in a sealed envelope. She looked at it awhile, then she leaned across and handed it to her mother.

"Do you really want me to read it for you?"

"You might as well."

Mrs. Hocker ripped the seal and pulled out the card. She read it to herself with that same slight smile tipping her lips. Then she said, "It says: 'Inside of every fat person, there's a thin one wildly signaling to be let out. . . . Here's to our thin selves, Susan. P. John.' "

"That's neat," Natalia said. "That's really neat."

Dinky didn't say anything.

Mrs. Hocker said, "It's an appropriate sentiment, and it's an appropriate gift. I quite approve."

"I'm glad you do," Dinky muttered.

"You see now, Dinky, why that gold watch was way out of proportion to the occasion?" Mrs. Hocker said.

Dinky didn't look up. She didn't answer. Marcus stopped blowing up the balloons. You could hear a pin drop. Dinky's face was very red.

Mrs. Hocker said, "You would have made a fool out of yourself, Dinky. I'm not trying to embarrass you. But you *and* your friends should appreciate the fact that I *do* know what's proper, and what isn't."

Mrs. Hocker glanced in Natalia's direction. "Do *you* see that I'm right, now? I know you didn't see it last night. You thought I was very hard on Dinky. But this *friend* of Dinky's—and that's *all* he ever was, a friend—was primarily interested in her weight problem."

Natalia sighed. Marcus looked away and began blowing up balloons again.

Mrs. Hocker continued, "This is a good lesson for all of us. We mustn't overrespond to people who take an interest in us. We must always keep things in perspective. A friend is just a friend."

"Except when your parents tell you he can't be your friend anymore," Dinky said.

"Not anymore, not at the door," Natalia said.

Mr. Hocker was carrying plates of food into the dining room.

"Dinky," Mrs. Hocker said, "I'll only say two more things on this subject. One is: I did not admire the particular friend in question. He was smug and narrow-minded. Two is: The particular friend in question did not admire you in the way you admired him. He was solely interested in exercising his authority over you."

Dinky gave a helpless shrug, staring down at the floor.

"He wasn't worthy of you, Sweetheart," Mrs. Hocker said.

"Supper is served! The Carollers are just down the street!" Mr. Hocker shouted from the dining room.

By this time the seven balloons were floating around the living room. Natalia and Marcus began poking them, reading them, and filling in sentences. Dinky got up and wandered toward the dining room. Tucker waited for Mrs. Hocker to enter the dining room before him.

Suddenly, she stopped.

She began to read aloud the words written on the balloons. "I think . . . I know . . . I want . . . I care . . . I need . . . I miss . . . I love."

She stared at Tucker momentarily.

"Supper is *served*," Mr. Hocker said. "Natalia, will you please help Dinky serve everyone?"

Natalia ran into the dining room with Marcus chasing her and poking a balloon in her direction.

Mrs. Hocker said to Tucker, "What did Dinky mean, Tucker, when she said the balloons are an inside joke?"

"They're a game," Tucker said. They were entering the dining room together.

"What kind of a game?"

"A word game."

"I want? I need? I love?"

"Yeah."

"I *want?* I *need?* I *love?*" Her tone of voice was edging on anger.

For a moment there was another heavy silence.

Then Dinky said, "I want you in bed. I need you in bed. I love you in bed. They sleep together, Mother."

"Oh, man!" Marcus laughed.

"Dinky, go to your room! You are not the least bit amusing. You are a *most* unpleasant little girl."

"I'm a most unpleasant big fat elephant!" Dinky said. She turned to Natalia. "I'm sorry you can't rhyme elephant, Natalia."

"Dinky!" Mr. Hocker barked. "Apologize!"

"Don't apologize to lies," Natalia said. She was standing in front of the buffet between the salad and the chili. Her face was pale.

"I won't apologize to lies," Dinky said. "Surprise, surprise."

Mrs. Hocker's temper snapped then. "You're not *better* than you think you are at all, Dinky! You're exactly like that Knight boy! Detestable! Detestable!"

"Dinky, go to your room," Mr. Hocker commanded. "Helen, calm down."

The "I love—" balloon floated down in front of Dinky. She smashed it with her hands.

Then she left.

"Let's all cool down," Mr. Hocker said.

"This is a swell-looking spread," Marcus said.

"Serve Marcus, please, Natalia," Mr. Hocker said.

"Tucker," said Mrs. Hocker, "you can explain your little inside joke to Mr. Hocker and me after supper."

"Will you please serve Marcus?" Mr. Hocker told Natalia.

Natalia looked from the chili to the salad, as though she were trying to decide which one to put on the plate first.

"I'm starved!" Marcus said.

"Serve Marcus," Mrs. Hocker said in a voice choking with rage.

Natalia did a strange thing then.

She took a large spoonful of the salad and put it on a plate. She took a large spoonful of chili and put it on top of the salad. Then she took two forks and mixed the salad and the chili together.

She handed the plate to Marcus.

She said, "It'll all end up that way eventually, won't it?"

Was she laughing or crying? Tucker couldn't tell.

Then while everyone was just standing there, staring at the plate Natalia had handed Marcus, Nader let out a yowl. She had sniffed the pepper on the poinsettia plant. She came flying through the dining room with her ruff up. She leaped over the table and clawed her way up Mrs. Hocker's drapes. She hung there screaming.

Outside, the Heights Carollers were singing: "Sing, choirs of angels,/Sing in exultation,/Sing, all ye citizens of heav'n above."

ELEVEN

The Leeds School
Leedston, Maine
December 27th

Dear Tucker,
This will be my new address as of the first of the year.
Actually, it is only about thirty miles from my aunt's, so I will be able to visit her when I want to.
My aunt is getting along in years (she is 55 now) and not as sharp a thinker as she used to be. She laughs and says she guesses she is mellowing in her old age, but like many Americans, she is going soft and fuzzy-headed.
She actually let some hippies use an acre of her land for a commune last summer. Not surprisingly, their crops failed. They were trying to

farm without using insecticides. Leeds School is her idea. It is run like a farm, and all the students have to share in the work. I'll believe that when I see it. Guess who'll probably be doing most of the work?

Please ask Mr. Baird to send me my poem about the Chinese in the UN, and my short story "Answered Prayers." He still has them. Leeds also has Creative Writing.

Please give the enclosed letter to Susan. How is she?

Best wishes,
P. John Knight

105 Joralemon Street
Brooklyn, New York
January 1

Dear P. John,

A lot has happened since I last saw you.

Christmas day at the Hockers turned into this big fiasco which is too complicated to go into. I didn't even get supper. I don't think anyone ate but Marcus. Everyone was fighting with everyone else, and I was told I can't see Natalia anymore. According to Mrs. Hocker, I upset her too much. So now we are both blacklisted.

Then when I was walking home from there, I saw all this black smoke coming from Montague Street. My uncle got drunk and fell asleep smoking a cigarette on this sleigh bed in our new health store. Our ex-health store now. We were wiped out.

Anyway, we are all going to church this morning and pray like mad for a miracle of some kind. I hope it won't turn out like your version of "Answered Prayers."

I haven't seen Susan or Natalia since Christmas. I'll get your letter to her somehow. She received your gift and really liked it.

I hope Leeds turns out to be a good place.

Best,

Tucker

"Almighty God," the minister intoned, "the fountain of all wisdom, who knowest our necessities before we ask, and our weaknesses before we sin; we beseech thee to forgive and have compassion upon our infirmities—"

Tucker opened one eye and looked in Jingle's direction. He could only see Jingle's profile. Jingle was kneeling with his elbows resting on the pew in front of him and his fingers at his mouth, as though he were biting his nails. His hands were bandaged to cover his burns, and there was a small bandage over his left eye. He was sitting on the aisle, next to Tucker's mother. Tucker sat between his mother and father. Tucker's father was barely speaking to Jingle.

Tucker couldn't decide whether Jingle's face looked so red because all the references to "weaknesses," "forgiveness," and "infirmities" embarrassed him, or whether Jingle just had the usual Sunday-morning hangover.

Dinky was sitting with her parents three pews ahead of the Woolfs. Natalia was not with them.

Tucker had not been able to get Dinky's eye, but after the Collect, when everyone rose to sing the Recessional, she glanced back at him.

Everyone was singing, ". . . Ring, happy bells, across the snow:/The year is going, let him go:/Ring out the false, ring in the true."

Dinky rolled her eyes to the rafters as if to say A-*men!*

"*Ring out the grief that saps the mind,*" Tucker's father sang with fierce conviction.

"*. . . Ring out the feud . . .*" Tucker's mother trilled ardently.

When the service was over, Dinky headed down the aisle toward Tucker.

"I'm sorry your store burned down, Mr. Woolf," she said.

"Thank you," Tucker's father said.

"Tucker, do you want to go for a walk?"

Tucker's mother answered for him. "Do you have your mother's permission, Dinky?" Tucker had told his mother a little bit about what had happened over at the Hockers' on Christmas day, but the fire had overshadowed everything.

"She has my permission, of course," Mrs. Hocker's voice came from behind Dinky. "Hello, Mr. and Mrs. Woolf. Hello, there, Tucker," she said sweetly, just as though Christmas day had never happened.

Tucker didn't even look over his shoulder at her. He didn't even answer her.

"You and Dinky go ahead," she purred. "We

aren't having dinner for another hour."

Mr. and Mrs. Hocker began telling Tucker's mother and father how sorry they were that Help Yourself burned down. Dinky grabbed Tucker's arm and pulled him down the aisle.

"Where's Natalia?" Tucker said.

"I'll get to that later," Dinky answered. "Right now my mind's on more important things."

When they got outside, she hurried so fast that Tucker had to jog along the icy pavements to keep up with her.

"Where are we going?" Tucker said.

"You'll see," she said turning down Henry Street.

They slipped and slid all the way down to Atlantic Avenue, until Dinky finally stopped before a small doorway.

The sign above the doorway said FRENCH RESTAURANT ATLANTIC.

It was a small wood-paneled room with a large globe light hanging from the ceiling over every table.

The waiter brought them menus when they sat down, and Tucker glanced at his, put it face down on the table, and said, "Shish kebab? Curry? What are we doing here? They're serving lunch!"

"I know what they're serving," Dinky said. "The menu's mostly Middle-Eastern, despite the sign out front."

"I thought we were going for a walk."

"We did, didn't we? Didn't we walk down here?"

"I can't even afford a Coke," Tucker complained. "Coke's sixty cents, for Pete's sake!"

"It's my treat," Dinky said. "I got money for Christmas."

"Is this what we almost broke our necks for?" Tucker said.

"This place fills up fast after church," Dinky said. "You didn't want to have to wait for a table, did you?"

"I didn't even want to come here," Tucker said.

"Order a crepe," Dinky told him. "The crepes are the only French thing on the menu." She turned around and told the waiter, "I'll have a baklava and a Turkish demitasse, and he'll have a raspberry crepe and a Coke."

Before Tucker could protest, she said, "We'll trade back and forth. Then you can taste the crepe *and* the pastry."

"Would it make any difference if I said I wasn't hungry?" Tucker said.

"It'd make a difference of about one thousand calories where I'm concerned," she answered. "Waste not, want not."

"I've got a letter for you," Tucker said reaching into his coat pocket for it. He placed it on the table. "It's from P. John."

Dinky didn't even pick it up.

"In case you're interested," she said, "Natalia is spending a few days at Renaissance House. She always goes back there when anything upsets her."

"How upset is she?" Tucker said.

"Time will tell. She's supposed to be back for school in three more days."

"What made her mix the food up that way?" Tucker said. "Was she just rattled?"

"She was the only one who made any sense that whole Christmas day," Dinky said. "It *does* all end up that way in your stomach, doesn't it? Everyone else was getting so basic, why shouldn't she?"

"Was *I* getting so basic?" Tucker said.

"Primitive is the word for you," Dinky said. "You were practically drooling with all those stupid balloons."

"I didn't mean them that way."

"My mother isn't interested in what *you* mean. She's interested in what *she* means, and you played right into her hands."

"Then how come she was so nice to me at church?"

"She's always nice in church. That's when she's at her best. There was a big fight Christmas night after you left. My father said she jumped to conclusions."

"That fight started before I left."

"It lasted all night," Dinky said. "My mother even dragged Natalia out of bed and made her explain your stupid balloon game."

"Does she believe that it was only a game, now?"

"Yes. But she says behind every game there's a deeper meaning."

"She's evil," Tucker said.

"Evil but not often wrong," Dinky said.

"Don't you want to read P. John's letter?"

"I'll read it when I get around to it. —Why is the service so slow in this place? A person could starve to death in this place."

"She's really wrong about P. John, Susan."

"Don't call me Susan anymore. It's laughable."

Then, abruptly, she changed the subject.

She told Tucker this long story about a one-armed man who was hanging around a lovers' lane in Prospect Park. There were rumors that he tried to get in the cars and carry off the girls. He banged on the windshields with his hooked wooden arm and frothed at the mouth. He only said two words: *bloody murder;* and his voice was high and hoarse.

Dinky claimed this girl who went to St. Marie's was up in Prospect Park one night with a boyfriend. The girl and her boyfriend began discussing the one-armed man while they were parked. They both got frightened and decided to leave. The boy dropped the girl off at her house, and drove home. When he got out of his car, he found this hook attached to his door handle.

Dinky said, "They must have driven off just as he was about to open the door."

"I thought you weren't interested in the bizarre, anymore," Tucker said.

"It's a true story."

"It's still bizarre."

"So is Nader, lately. She's gone wild. She's changed overnight."

"So have you," Tucker said.

"I haven't changed," Dinky said as the waitress

130

brought their order. "I've changed *back*. I'm my normal self again."

She dug into the baklava. "Try the crepe," she said.

Tucker didn't eat anything. He took a sip of Coke and said, "I think I really hate your mother."

"She's crude, but she speaks the truth," Dinky said.

"I wish you'd read P. John's letter."

"Read it yourself," she said. "It won't say anything you'd want to print on a balloon."

"He wrote it to *you*," Tucker said.

"He's power-mad. He's a fascist."

"You don't even know what a fascist is," Tucker said.

"A fascist doesn't care about the individual. He only cares about a cause—like Weight Watchers."

She pushed the letter in front of Tucker. "Read it and see," she said. "Read it aloud."

Tucker tore open the envelope and began reading:

Dear Susan,
I'll be at the above address as of January 1.
Don't give up the WW meetings just because I'm away.

"You see?" Dinky interrupted. "He's a Jean Nidetch fascist."

"Who's Jean Nidetch?"

"The Weight Watchers' dictator. She dresses all in white and carries one red rose. I've seen pictures of her. She once weighed 214 pounds."

Tucker continued with the letter:

More people die in the United States of too much food than of too little.

"My mother's right," Dinky said, starting in on the crepe. "He's not a sympathetic character. He doesn't realize people are starving in the United States."

"*You're* not," Tucker said.

"I was a minute ago."

"Very funny," Tucker said sarcastically.

If you want to correspond about things, you have my address and Tucker could pass along my answers.

It was an odd sort of Christmas, wasn't it?

We could let each other know how many pounds we lose every week.

I'd really like to know how you're doing.

Maybe it's too much trouble writing back and forth, considering the big hassle with our parents.

I'm much better off where I am.

Sincerely,
P. John Knight

"Oh my my my my my," Dinky exclaimed, sounding exactly like her mother. "Isn't *that* romantic."

TWELVE

THE THIRD week in January, Tucker's father began a new job in public relations, at half the salary he was accustomed to.

That same week, on Friday night, he invited Jingle to dinner. It was the first time Jingle had been to the town house since the fire.

"Your mother's working late, so we'll get everything ready," Tucker's father said when he got home from the office.

Stirring Romances was doing a special June issue on unmarried mothers. A banner for the cover was to proclaim "WE WERE NEVER BRIDES," and all the stories were supposed to be confessions of young women who'd found unhappiness in breaking the rules of society.

Tucker's mother had been working overtime for days to "get the book to bed," which was magazine jargon for finishing a complete issue and shipping it off to the printer.

Tucker's father was trying to teach him how to make a meat loaf. They were moving around the kitchen clumsily, bumping into each other and making a mess.

"We haven't had a chance to talk together in a long time," Tucker's father said, wiping up some ketchup he had spilled on the floor. "This will be good for us."

Tucker put a Band-Aid on his finger where he'd cut himself slicing onions. He said, "How do you like the new job?"

"It's too easy, and it's not enough money," his father said. "But I hope it'll work into something more important."

"What time is Jingle coming by?" Tucker said.

"In about an hour," his father said. "I suppose we should have bought a portable fire extinguisher."

"You're really good-natured, Dad," Tucker said. "There were two things I never thought you'd do: ask Jingle here again, and take a job you weren't really excited about."

His father opened a package of chopped steak and dumped it into a bowl. "Tucker," he said, "to make anything work, from a meat loaf to a marriage, there are two things you *have* to do. Forgive and continue."

"I'll try to remember that," Tucker said.

"It's worth remembering, son. And there's something else I want you to do."

"What's that?"

"From now on, I want you to feel like an equal around here."

"I feel like an equal," Tucker said, thinking his father was about to apologize again for not spending much time with him in the past three months.

"Good," his father said. "Then you won't mind getting dinner now and then, or doing the dishes, or running the vacuum cleaner through the house. Your mother's going to make an announcement tonight, and everything I'm saying now is pertinent to what she's going to announce."

"What's she going to announce?"

"She wants to tell you herself. I'm all for it, and I think you will be, too. But we've all got to pull together from here on in, Tucker."

"We're really broke, aren't we?" Tucker said.

"We're not rich, if that's what you mean."

"Not even close," Tucker said.

"No, not even close," his father agreed. "Now watch what I'm going to do with the egg and breadcrumbs."

It wasn't a pretty sight. His father mixed everything up with his hands: the meat, the ketchup, the egg, the breadcrumbs, the onions, the green pepper, and the chopped peanuts.

"Are you sure about the peanuts?" Tucker asked.

"The peanuts are my special touch," his father answered. "You can use celery, or mushrooms; or celery, mushrooms, *and* peanuts. The trick is to stretch your food dollar."

"Maybe I should get a job," Tucker said.

"I thought of that," his father said, "but you'll be of more use helping around here. We're not going to have a cleaning woman anymore, and there'll be nights both your mother and I will be getting home late. We're going to depend on you a lot."

"You're actually going to eat what I cook?" Tucker said.

"You're going to have to eat it, too," his father said, "so bone up."

Jingle arrived with a bottle of red wine just as they were putting the meat loaf into the oven.

"This is not my sole peace offering," he announced as he set the bottle down on the table. "I have also brought along my guts, all neatly typed and bound in a play manuscript. After dinner, I'll read it aloud."

"The more things change, the more they remain the same," Tucker's father said.

But things around the Joralemon Street town house were not going to stay the same. When Tucker's mother came home she made the big announcement: Beginning in February, she was going to attend night classes at Brooklyn Law School.

"Bless my dark and sinister soul!" Jingle exclaimed over the news. "Here come de judge!"

After dinner, Jingle read his play. It was about a man in hell. Hell was one room with a mirror in it, and nothing else. While the man sat before the mirror, his reflection reviewed his entire life in minute detail, pointing out everything he'd done wrong.

The play was called, *Now It's My Turn To Talk*.

It was a very long play, and Jingle began reading it almost immediately after Tucker's mother had told everyone her news.

She hadn't even had a chance to go into detail —to say what courses she was going to take, or what kind of a lawyer she wanted to be, or how long it was going to take.

Tucker felt like shouting out, "Bore-*ring!*" in the middle of Jingle's reading, and he felt bad about the way his mother had simply been cut off by Jingle. But his mother sat listening to Jingle's play with this earnest expression on her face, while Tucker's father leaned back with his eyes closed, breathing very deeply.

Tucker remembered what his father had told him earlier: Forgive and continue.

* * *

It was a Friday afternoon. While Tucker was walking along Montague Street, he heard a familiar voice say, "How *are* you, Tucker?"

"Fine, Mrs. Hocker. Just fine."

"You're exactly the person I wanted to see today," she said.

Tucker felt like walking away, but he had to admit his father's philosophy was practical, even if it wasn't likely to revolutionize the world. It *was* okay for meat loaf, marriage, and meeting Mrs. Hocker on Montague Street.

"What did you want to see me about?" Tucker said.

Since that day after church, Tucker had not laid eyes on Dinky or heard any news of Natalia.

"You know how to draw, don't you?" Mrs. Hocker asked.

"Yes. I can draw."

"I have a new little afternoon group of ghetto children I'm working with, Tucker. We meet on Tuesdays at the parish house of the church. What we need is an artist to help us."

"I'm not an artist, Mrs. Hocker."

"Could you drop by next Tuesday at four?" she continued, ignoring his disclaimer. "I want to start them finger-painting and watercoloring. You could help us get started. These are *very* poor children, Tucker. They've had none of your advantages. Some of them don't even have heat in their homes on cold days like these, and—"

"I get it," Tucker interrupted.

"Will you do us this favor, dear?"

"How's Natalia?" Tucker said.

"Oh, she'll be there, dear. Dinky and Natalia are helping, too."

Tucker just stared at her, as though she were an amnesia victim and one of the things she'd forgotten was Christmas day.

Mrs. Hocker got the message.

She said, "I'm going to give you another chance, Tucker. I'm going to trust you to see Natalia without upsetting her."

Tucker felt like telling her she could take her trust and shove it.

Mrs. Hocker said, "I had a long talk with a psychologist who knows Natalia very well. He thinks it's important for her to have friends. Not just the girls she meets at St. Marie's, but other friends, too."

"Boyfriends," Tucker said.

"Boys, who are also friends. Yes," Mrs. Hocker said. "Will you be there, Tucker? Can we count on you?"

"All right," Tucker said. "But I've never finger-painted in my life."

"The ghetto children won't know that," Mrs. Hocker promised. "Most of them don't even own a box of crayons."

At that point Dinky materialized, carrying two chocolate-dip cones from the King George Ice Cream Parlor. She was licking one and holding the other. Tucker thought at first that she was bringing the other to Mrs. Hocker, but she wasn't. Tucker looked around to see if Natalia was with her.

Dinky read his mind. "They're both for me," she said. "I'm supposed to gorge myself before I start this new diet tomorrow. I'm going to be injected with a hormone they make from pregnant women's urine."

Mrs. Hocker winced. *"Dinky!"* she said. "Ladies don't discuss intimate details like that!"

"It's true, though," Dinky said. "It's called Follutin. Every injection costs five dollars. I'll be getting a fix every day."

"What is it about you, Tucker," Mrs. Hocker said, "that makes Dinky want to say unnecessary things?"

Tucker stood there trying to dream up an unnecessary answer, when Dinky suddenly changed the subject. "Did you tell him about Nader, mother? Tucker, she's giving Nader to the A.S.P.C.A."

"Only if we can't find a new home for her," Mrs. Hocker said.

"You know what they do with cats at the A.S.P.C.A.? They gas them," Dinky said. "So much for the prevention of cruelty to animals."

THIRTEEN

TUESDAY AFTERNOON Tucker worked with the children in the basement of the church house from three thirty to four thirty. The only one who really painted on the paper Mrs. Hocker supplied was Marcus. He was helping Tucker. The kids themselves had painted their fingers, their faces, their clothes, and the floor.

Marcus had painted a rainbow with a jug at the end labeled POT.

"That's a pot of gold," he told Tucker. "The other kind of pot messes up your brain, man."

"Speaking of pots," Tucker said, "I have to go home and make dinner."

"That's heavy. "What're you going to cook?"

"I don't know," Tucker said. He began helping the kids clean up, while Marcus described how everyone at DRI took turns cooking. Marcus said his specialty was Mushroom Dream.

"You take a can of mushroom soup, a can of tuna fish, and a can of peas," Marcus said. "Mix them all together in a casserole, sprinkle some grated cheese on top, and put it in the oven for half an hour."

Then Tucker saw Natalia.

"Just double the recipe if you're cooking for four," Marcus said, "and triple it if you're cooking for six."

Natalia was helping one of the older kids find her coat.

Tucker walked over to the coat rack and said, "Hello."

"Hello, Tucker," Natalia said. Tucker had never seen her in jeans. She wore an old red-flannel shirt; her hair was pulled back and held with a red ribbon. She no longer had an old-fashioned look. She looked just like one of the St. Marie girls now, only prettier than most of them.

She said, "This is Wendy, Tucker. We just made a collage."

Wendy was around eight. She handed Tucker the collage. It was made on an old newspaper. A piece of red felt was pasted to the newspaper in the shape of a candle. A piece of yellow felt was attached like a flame. Letters of various shapes and colors formed the words: PSALMS xviii.28.

Tucker said, "What does that mean?"

"Mrs. Hocker wanted our collages to have a biblical theme," Natalia said. "Psalms xviii.28 says, 'For thou wilt light my candle.' "

"I've missed you," Tucker said.

" 'For thou wilt light my candle: the Lord my God will enlighten my darkness,' " Wendy rattled off.

"Are you leaving now?" Tucker said. "I'm leaving now. I could walk you home."

"I think Dinky has something to tell you," Natalia said.

"Then can I walk you home?"

Natalia nodded.

Upstairs, Dinky was in the process of finishing a large collage she was making with a twelve-year-old black boy named William. There was a pile of magazines on the floor beside them. They were working on a large sheet of light blue paper cutting out pictures of people yawning or sleeping and pasting it to the paper. They had also pasted on words like "Ho hum!" "Boring!" "Snore!" "Groan!" and "So What!"

"What biblical theme is that?" Tucker asked William.

"Don't tell him until we're through," Dinky said. "We'll be through in a minute or two, as soon as I paste on the Bible verse." Then she said, "You have to take Nader, Tucker. She has to be out by tonight!"

"I can't take her and you know it," Tucker said.

"Then she's going to her final reward, over at the A.S.P.C.A. gas chamber."

"You're pretty calm about it," Tucker said.

"One thing I'm not, these days, is calm," Dinky said.

"That's true," Natalia said.

"Here's a 13," William said, handing it to Dinky to paste after a word "Hebrews."

"Now look for an 8," Dinky told him. She said to Tucker, "I'm not taking those injections, after all. My father didn't want me shooting up. I'm on Preludin, instead, and it keeps me hopped up, so don't call me calm about anything, but Nader has to go."

"Don't talk so fast," Tucker said.

"Don't tell me how fast to talk," Dinky said. "My motor's running."

"What's Preludin?" Tucker said.

"They're diet pills. They take away my appetite. I'm going to lose twenty-five pounds by Valentine's Day. Tell that to the storm trooper in Maine."

"What's Nader done?" Tucker said.

"Her motor's running, too. She's peeing on everything in sight."

"You shouldn't say someone's peeing," William said. "You should say someone's going to the bathroom."

"Well, she's not going to the bathroom," Dinky told him. "That's the whole point."

"Here's an 8," William said.

"Paste it on," Dinky said.

"I can't take Nader," Tucker said.

"Maybe they won't gas her," Dinky said. "I hear they sell some to hospitals so they can experiment on them. I hear they perform these gruesome experiments on helpless animals in the name of science. First they dip them in boiling water and then they dip them in freezing water, I hear, and sometimes they skin them alive."

"You shouldn't be talking like that," William said. "I shouldn't be listening to stuff like this, I don't think."

"Listen, William, it's a tough world," Dinky said. "If you don't speak out, you get the shaft. Remember that. An animal can't speak out, so unless someone takes pity on it, it gets the shaft. It's the same with some people. The meek don't inherit the earth, I don't care what the Bible says. The meek inherit the shaft."

"Don't tell him that," Natalia said.

"Why shouldn't I tell him the truth?" Dinky said. "You yourself never got anyplace until you started rhyming. Why do you think you had to rhyme that way? To get attention!"

"Don't mention attention," Natalia said.

"Don't get nervous just because I'm stating a few facts of life," said Dinky. "Life isn't anything to get nervous about; it's something to get furious at."

She held up the finished collage. Superimposed across the pictures of everyone sleeping and yawning, and the words: "Ho hum!" "Boring!" "Snore!" "Groan!" and "So What!" was:

HEBREWS 13:8

"Is it done?" William said.

145

"Right," Dinky said. "Our biblical theme is boredom."

"There's nothing about boredom in the Bible," Tucker said.

"How would you know?" Dinky said. "My mother says you and your family only show up in church once a year."

"You're in a nice mood today," Tucker said.

"Preludin never promised anyone a rose garden," Dinky said. "It makes you more alert, so you see all the flyspecks and dog-doo in life. It takes away your appetite for more than just food."

"It takes away your mood," Natalia said.

"Oh, stop rhyming. It's just as boring as Hebrews 13:8 says everything is."

"What *does* Hebrews 13:8 say, anyway?" Tucker said.

"It's my new motto," Dinky answered. " 'Jesus Christ the same yesterday, and to-day, and for ever.' "

Tucker walked Natalia back to the Hockers', and on the way Natalia began to cry.

"She didn't really mean what she said about your rhyming," Tucker said.

Natalia didn't answer.

"She's just very unhappy," Tucker said. "She's just really angry. Remember that day she said a psychologist told her fat people had anger bottled up in them?"

Natalia nodded.

"Well, it's coming out now," Tucker said.

Natalia blew her nose on a Kleenex.

Tucker said, "I'll take Nader home with me. My father will have a fit, but I can't do anything else, can I?"

"N-no," Natalia managed.

"I get nervous, too," Tucker said. "When I get nervous, I go to the library and hang around. The libraries are filled with people who are nervous. You can blend in with them there. You're bound to see someone more nervous than you are in a library. Sometimes the librarians themselves are more nervous than you are. I'll probably be a librarian for that reason. Then if I'm nervous on the job, it won't show. I'll just stamp books and look up things for people and run back and forth to the staff room sneaking smokes until I get hold of myself. A library is a great place to hide."

Natalia said, "I have trouble with one-to-one relationships." She blurted it out very fast, as though she might not have said it at all if she'd hesitated.

"I have trouble with relationships in general," Tucker said. "I don't even think I have any relationships."

"Everyone has them," Natalia said softly.

"I don't think *I* do," Tucker said. "I have parents and I have a few friends, but I don't have relationships. I mean, my parents tell me what to do and I do it. And I tell my friends what I've done and they tell me what they've done. Are those relationships? No one even asks me my opinion on anything."

"I would," Natalia said.

"On what would you ask my opinion?" Tucker said. "On what?"

Natalia shrugged.

"Right," Tucker said. "There's no answer to that question. I have no style."

"*I* like you," Natalia said.

"Why?" Tucker said.

"Because of everything you just said," Natalia said. "That's neat. I don't think I have any relationships, either. All the time I've been worrying about one-to-one relationships, but I've never had one, either, probably. So there's nothing to worry about."

"*We* certainly don't have a relationship of any kind," Tucker said. "We couldn't even make conversation that night we were out with Susan and P. John."

"I know it," Natalia said.

"We've never even had a conversation unless we were writing inside balloons, or Susan was with us."

"That's really true," Natalia said.

"Susan and P. John had more of a relationship than we ever did. We're basically inadequate."

"I *always* was," Natalia said.

"I'm just too young to date, I guess," Tucker said. "I lack pizazz."

"That's neat," Natalia said.

"To lack pizazz?"

"To know it," Natalia said. "Once you know it, you don't have to pretend anymore. You can just relax. You don't have to have relationships."

"I'll have to think about all this," Tucker said.

They had arrived at the Hockers'.

Mrs. Hocker must have been peering at them through the venetian blinds, because she came to the door and opened it while they were standing out front. "Come in, come in," she said. "It's warmer in here than out there."

"I just came to get Nader," Tucker said.

"What about your father's allergy, Tucker?" Mrs. Hocker said.

"I don't know," Tucker said. "We'll just have to see how long it takes to find her a new home."

Natalia said, "Maybe a new girl will take Nader now."

Tucker heard what she said, but there was something about her tone of voice that made him react as though he hadn't heard, a sadness of some sort. He said, "What?"

"Nothing," Natalia said.

They were standing there looking at each other, with Mrs. Hocker between them, under the bright light in the foyer.

"What does it matter, anyway?" Tucker said, answering her remark then about the new girl, while they both stared at each other. She didn't look away from his face for a long moment, and in the meantime Tucker had this feeling that something was happening to them. What he felt was this punch to his insides while their faces were fixed on each other.

When she finally dropped her glance, he felt weak-kneed.

"What does it matter, anyway?" she repeated what he had said.

"I *said* that." His voice was strangely hoarse.

"I know," she almost whispered.

"Natalia," Mrs. Hocker said, "get Nader's carrying case."

Tarrying place, burying place, marrying face, Tucker thought while he stood there watching Natalia walk down the hall, *what's happening to me, anyway?*

Before Tucker went home with Nader, he stopped on Montague Street and picked up the ingredients for Mushroom Dream and a large bag of cat litter.

He fixed Nader's pan, and then he made the casserole and put it in the oven.

He sat down and read a letter which was waiting for him from P. John.

It was hard to concentrate on the letter, because he kept trying to remember his conversation with Natalia.

The one time they had had a conversation alone together, and he could hardly remember it.

He could close his eyes, though, and get back some of the feeling that had been there in the foyer. It was a completely physical feeling, but the strange part about it was that it didn't seem to be a sexual feeling. It wasn't the kind of sensation he had sometimes after reading sexy parts in novels, or while seeing sexy photographs, nor was it like feelings he had after sexy daydreams.

It was just this strong feeling, completely physical, done with eyes.

Eyes.

Nader was tearing around the house knocking things off tables, and Tucker finally caught her, held her on his lap, and talked to her.

She fell asleep eventually and Tucker, too, calmed down long enough to see what P. John had to say:

Dear Tucker,

Did you give my letter to Susan or not? I haven't heard from her. I haven't heard much from my father, either, so I guess he's still angry with me. Dewey can't even get bail, though I heard Mr. Hocker tried his best.

At Leeds we are divided into two teams every month. I am on the management team this month. We try to direct the labor team, which is supposed to do most of the chores. Like labor anywhere, they are lazy and demanding, but I am in charge of management mediation and I know how to be tough. It's really good experience, though I have very little time to work on my writing. There are so many disputes to settle! I get a lot of satisfaction out of putting my ideas to the test.

I'm not even trying to diet, and I'm losing weight.

How is Susan doing? Is she in WW or not?

I'm not particularly broken-hearted because she hasn't written, but I wonder if she got my letter, that's all.

We have girls at Leeds, too, but I haven't met one yet I like that much.

Are Susan's parents still down on me? I suppose they are. Are you still blacklisted, too?

A political science course here actually assigns one of my father's books. But they read conservative thinkers, too, so no one is brainwashed. I was just surprised they assign him.

Best wishes,
P. John Knight

FOURTEEN

THAT FRIDAY, the Hockers and Natalia were invited to dinner. Tucker's mother was eager to talk with Mr. Hocker about her class in Constitutional Law. Tucker's father agreed to let Tucker, Natalia and Dinky prepare everything, providing Mushroom Dream was not on the menu.

When Natalia arrived with the groceries around five that afternoon, Dinky was not with her.

"She's being punished," Natalia said. "She got William in trouble at his Sunday School, and his mother called Aunt Helen about it."

Tucker took the Bohack bag from her arms and began unloading it.

He said, "How did she get William in trouble? Was it the collage?"

"No. She kept the collage."

"Then how did she get him in trouble?"

"She taught him this riddle."

"Go on," Tucker said, "what riddle?"

"It's not very nice," Natalia said. Then she laughed and covered her mouth with her hand quickly, as though her laughter had been an accident. She said, "Actually it's just a play on words. I mean, it isn't a *bad* word. It doesn't mean anything bad. But it goes against the rules, you know?"

"No, I don't know," Tucker said. "Just tell me the riddle."

"Okay," Natalia said, "but it isn't my riddle."

"Just tell me."

"Okay," Natalia said. "What was the slipperiest day in Bethlehem?"

"I give up."

"It was the day Joseph came through on his ass."

"I see what you mean," Tucker grinned.

"Ass means buttocks, and there's nothing wrong with buttocks unless you call them your ass. If ass is only supposed to mean donkey, then it shouldn't be in the dictionary that it also means buttocks. Do you agree with me, Tucker?"

"No," Tucker said, "because the dictionary doesn't dictate what words are proper or improper —it just tells you what words are in use."

"Then how did ass get to be an improper word for buttocks?"

"It's all tied in with sex," Tucker said. "When they made the rules, they decided any part of your body that isn't supposed to show isn't supposed to be called by a slang name. Parts of your body that

154

you don't show are supposed to be connected with sex."

"Is that it?"

"I don't know," Tucker said. "There are probably lots of things wrong with that argument, but it's the best I can come up with, off the top of my head."

All the while Tucker was setting the groceries out on the kitchen table, he was wondering why he didn't feel the way he had felt a few nights ago. Before Natalia had arrived, he hadn't been able to do his chemistry homework or answer P. John's letter, or finish the J. D. Salinger short story he was reading, because he was too excited. But now that Natalia was there, he just felt like his old self, a little happier than usual.

"We're having Spaghetti Carbonara," Natalia said. "That's spaghetti with bacon, butter, chives and grated cheese mixed into it. It's my father's recipe, only he used to put a raw egg on top. Yiiik!" She made a face, and Tucker pretended he was going to heave, bending forward with his tongue out.

Nader jumped up on the table and sniffed the bacon.

"She's still here!" Natalia said.

"My father's allergy is gone," Tucker said. "My mother said he wasn't allergic to the cat, he was allergic to being out of work."

"His symptoms were psychosomatic," Natalia said. "We had a girl at Renaissance who used to get migraine headaches whenever her mother visited."

"Migraines," Tucker said. "Not migraine headaches. Migraine means headache." He sounded the way his mother used to sound, but now his mother was into discussions of torts, liens, venue, statutes of limitation, and you-name-it.

"She used to get migraines," Natalia said. "A lot of things are psychosomatic. After my father killed himself, I couldn't talk for a long time. Then I could only talk if I rhymed."

"I guess you've been through a lot," Tucker said.

"He went through a lot, too," Natalia said. "That's the thing."

"What's the thing?"

"He was going through a lot and I didn't even realize it. I was just all full of myself, embarrassed because my mother had a mental illness, and worried that the kids were talking about me at school."

"They probably were," Tucker said.

"Oh, they were. But I didn't even realize what my father was going through. He really loved my mother and he couldn't help her—and I couldn't help him, because I was so conceited."

"Conceited?" Tucker said.

"Conceit masquerading as an inferiority complex," Natalia said. "If I'd really felt inferior, I wouldn't have devoted all my time to worrying over what kind of impression I was making. You have to be awfully conceited to concentrate on yourself day and night."

"I never thought of that," Tucker said, "but it's true. In my own case, I didn't even have any idea my mother had any ambition to be anything but my mother. She took this temporary job when my father was fired and I thought she couldn't wait to get back to just being my mother again. What she really couldn't wait to do was *stop* being just a mother. She wants to be something more important."

"I know," Natalia said. "That's neat."

"It is neat," Tucker said, "because she's been stuck being just my mother for fifteen years. I suppose that was important when I was little, but what good would it do her in three more years when I go to college?"

" 'Dear Tucker,' " Natalia said, " 'This is just your mother writing you again for the third time this week to ask how is my son.' "

"Exactly," Tucker said. "I don't know why I didn't see it before."

"That's why I never want to get married and have children until I'm very old," Natalia said. "The minute you get married and become a parent, you're nobody. You're just somebody's mother."

"I may never get married," Tucker said. "From what I've seen of myself, I don't want children."

"You're not so bad."

"How can you live with someone under the same roof for fifteen years," Tucker said, "and never have a clue that she wants to be important?"

"My father blew his brains out," Natalia said.

Tucker didn't have any answer for that.

There was a long silence.

"I've never said that out loud," Natalia said.

"I'm sorry," Tucker managed.

"So am I," Natalia said, "but I think I'll be able to handle it." She turned to Tucker and smiled slightly. " 'I am better than I think. A-one, a-two, a-three.' "

Tucker imitated Mrs. Hocker's falsetto: " 'We shouldn't be thinking how much better we are, Natalia, but how blessed we are.' "

Then while they were both laughing very hard, that same thing happened again, all done with eyes, and suddenly they had stopped laughing. You could hear the kitchen clock ticking. You could hear the furnace going in the basement. It was the longest moment and the shortest moment, and sometime during it, the outside buzzer rang.

And rang.

"That's probably my father," Tucker said finally, with effort. "He always forgets his key."

"You'd better answer it," Natalia said, as though they had a choice.

"I wouldn't believe it was the same animal," Mrs. Hocker said after dinner, while they were all sitting around in the living room watching Nader sleep on the radiator cover. "She's as docile as the day she arrived at our place. Of course she's still overweight."

"It's too bad Dinky couldn't come tonight," Tucker's mother said. "Don't you think she's been punished enough, Helen? Shouldn't Tucker telephone her and invite her over?"

Mr. Hocker said, "I think so, Helen, don't you?"

"In a way, it's my own fault," Mrs. Hocker said. "I allowed our family physician to prescribe diet pills for Dinky. Very mild ones. In my opinion, Dinky's just in a typical, adolescent plump stage, but she became self-conscious about it after meeting that Knight boy."

"Eric Establishment," Tucker's father said.

"Yes," Mrs. Hocker chuckled, "Eric Establishment. His father is actually a *very* liberal, *decent* man. At any rate, the pills had a bad effect on Dinky. She became extremely high-strung and irritable, rebellious, crass, not at all our daughter."

"We've forbidden her to take any more," Mr. Hocker said. "She'll just have to count calories or push herself away from the table—that's the best exercise, they say." He chortled and glanced across at his wife. "Shall we let her come, Helen?"

"All right," Mrs. Hocker said. "You may call her, Tucker."

"Tucker," Mr. Hocker said as he got up from his chair, "before you do, I want to make a public statement."

"What's that?" Tucker asked.

"I just want to say simply how pleased I am that you and Natalia and Dinky are all friends."

"I'm glad Natalia and Susan are my friends, too," said Tucker.

"You can come over," Tucker told Dinky when

she answered the phone. "Your mother's given you her permission."

"I heard something really weird," Dinky said. "Marcus called up and told me something fantastic about this ex-intern who joined DRI this week. He's hooked on morphine."

"That's not so weird," Tucker said. "A lot of doctors get hooked on morphine."

"That's not the weird part," Dinky said. "The weird part is this nurse at his hospital. She was a real uptight bitch. She was a snob. She'd tell on everybody and make trouble, and they all decided to get even with her."

"Come on over and tell us," Tucker said.

"Don't interrupt my story. These interns decided to freak her out. They were dissecting this corpse in their lab at the time. They took a hand off this corpse and sneaked inside this nurse's house with it. They attached the hand to a light switch. When she went home alone that night and reached out to turn on the lights—*zap!* The next morning they found her dead of a heart attack on the floor."

"Are you coming over or aren't you?" Tucker said.

"I can't," she said. "I just ordered a large Sicilian pizza with anchovies and cheese from Fascati."

"Come over after you eat it," Tucker said.

"Did you ever eat a large Sicilian pizza with anchovies and cheese and try to move after?"

"I heard from P. John," Tucker said. "He's losing weight."

"Don't try to humiliate me," Dinky said. "It won't work."

"He asked about you."

"Tell him if he wants to know my medical history, he can write our family doctor."

"You're in a bad mood," Tucker said.

"I'm hungry."

"Then you won't come by?"

"All the derricks are in use tonight. I have no transportation."

"I hope you change your mind," Tucker said. "We miss you."

"You don't miss me, so don't lie," Dinky said. "Tell my mother Marcus has been trying to get in touch with her all night. Tell her to call him at DRI. She'll be more interested in that than in my presence there, anyway."

There was a click and a dial tone.

Tucker gave Mrs. Hocker Dinky's message. Then he played a John Prine album for Natalia, while his father and mother and Mr. Hocker sat over in a far corner of the living room discussing Brooklyn Law School.

Tucker and Natalia listened to Prine sing his song, "Spanish Pipedream." It was all about blowing up your television set, throwing away your newspaper, and moving to the country to build a little home.

Mrs. Hocker came running into the room after she'd made her telephone call, and said, "Horace, there's an emergency, I'm afraid."

"What happened, dear?"

"It's Marcus," Mrs. Hocker said. "He's high."

"Where did he get it?" Mr. Hocker said.

"Does it matter?" Mrs. Hocker said. "The point is, he's at DRI, and he's upsetting everyone."

"They know how to handle him there," Mr. Hocker said.

"Horace," Mrs. Hocker said, "he needs *me*."

"Here we go again," Mr. Hocker sighed, but he got up, and he went to the hall for their coats.

That night when Tucker walked Natalia home, he kissed her.

It wasn't much of a kiss. It was a kiss on the mouth, lasting just long enough for Tucker to think the words, *I really feel something for you, Natalia*, which he had planned to say after the kiss.

But he didn't say anything, and he didn't really have a chance to feel anything, because while he was kissing her, he opened his eyes. Over Natalia's shoulder, he saw Dinky peering through the venetian-blind slats in the Hockers' living room.

"St. Marie's is having a Valentine dance in ten days," Natalia said after the kiss. "Would you be my date, Tucker?"

"Yes," Tucker said, which was more or less the beginning of their relationship.

FIFTEEN

April 14th

Dear Tucker,

Thanks for seeing that Mr. Baird mailed me my poem and story. They finally arrived! Not that I needed them for anything because I've been busy these past months organizing strikes. I am now a permanent member of the labor team. Normally, at Leeds, you are supposed to switch back and forth from labor to management, but I petitioned for an exception and won.

The thing is labor can't be effective as long as management sits around on its fat behind enjoying privileges half of them didn't even work to earn! I discovered that when it was management's turn to do hard labor, they goofed off and left the chores for the next rotation. No one really wanted to be on the labor team . . . and no wonder! It's hard work, long hours, no real compensation.

I volunteered to lead labor permanently (or did I say that already?), until the inequities are balanced out.

Right now we're striking again, which gives me time to write—when I'm not on duty in the picket line.

We're winning, because the school can't really function without us on the job.

It's hard to explain, but I'm beginning to form a new outlook. I've organized a strong union, with workmen's compensation and even welfare benefits for hardship cases.

I'm doing a term paper on Dewey's case. My father has sent me lots of material.

How's everything? Is Susan still around?

> *All the best,*
> *P. John Knight*

SIXTEEN

THAT SPRING, sometimes Tucker's mother would study until three or four in the morning, and then report to *Stirring Romances* by nine thirty.

Once Tucker found her hunched over some work, crying, at the kitchen table just as dawn was breaking. He had awakened to go to the bathroom, and at first he thought she was asleep sitting up. Then he saw her shoulders shaking. He went up behind her and looked down at the papers spread out in front of her. On one side were the page proofs of a manuscript called "I Married the Devil: He Wanted Me To Sleep in a Coffin." On the other side were long yellow sheets marked with headings like "Ancillary jurisdiction of federal courts and the basis thereof," and "Implied judicial power."

"Mom?" he said, reaching out to touch her shoulder. "Are you okay?"

"It's hard, honey. It's so hard," she answered. Then she bawled in great wails, hanging on to him for a long time.

But there were days when he had never seen her so happy, and his father had this strange new way with her, almost as though he were courting her all over again. He would bring her flowers and breakfast in bed on Sunday mornings; Saturdays he and Tucker would clean the house from top to bottom, and the few times they had company, his father would turn into this bore, bragging about her to the guests, and asking her to explain legal points she had already explained to him when they were alone.

"She's really smart, though," Tucker did his own share of bragging about her to Natalia. "She's really going to make it."

"Aunt Helen says she's a credit to the community," Natalia answered.

"Who cares about the community?" Tucker said. "She's not doing it for the community. She's doing it for herself."

"Aunt Helen cares about the community, to answer your question," Natalia said. "She says everything we do reflects on the community."

It was an afternoon in late April. They were at DRI headquarters, where Tucker was helping to set up a library. Natalia was organizing the poetry section for it.

Tucker was working there after school, two afternoons a week. Then he would go home and prepare dinner. Since February he had learned to make beef stew, baked beans, goulash, Spanish rice, and corned beef and cabbage. His father was the gourmet cook in the family now. When Tucker wasn't cooking, Cal Woolf made things like Sweetbreads Albert and Swiss enchiladas.

"Aunt Helen's going to get an award," Natalia said.

"I heard all about it," Tucker said. "The Heights Samaritan Award. My family's been invited to the banquet."

"I'm glad," Natalia said. "She's been upset ever since Marcus slipped."

"He didn't slip, he recidivated," Tucker said.

"She put in a lot of work on Marcus."

"She always puts in a lot of work on other people," Tucker said. "Meanwhile, how's Susan?"

"I've never seen her so interested in anything as her aquarium," Natalia said. "I just wish she wouldn't keep her microworms in the refrigerator."

When a new store called Aquarium Plus opened on the corner of Clinton and Joralemon, Dinky began spending all her time in there. First she bought a one-gallon aquarium and filled it with guppies; then she bought a five-gallon aquarium and filled it with swordtails, platys, and dwarf cichlids.

For her birthday in March, her father bought her a twenty-gallon aquarium. She filled it with everything from zebra danios to angelfish.

Her bedroom looked like a dark nightclub for fish.

Dinky spent most of her time in there watching

them, listening to her vast collection of records, and devouring Sara Lee cakes.

Tucker had peered in at her one Friday night, when he had gone to the Hockers' to pick up Natalia. They were going down to the Heights Cinema I to see a new movie and Tucker had asked Dinky to join them.

"I can't," she told him. "My cichlids are spawning."

She was sitting in the dark on a large leather hassock before a tank with green lights, the tank was swimming with fish and corkscrew tape grass.

"Let them spawn," Tucker said. "You'll only be gone a few hours, for Pete's sake."

"You don't know anything about cichlid spawning behavior," Dinky said. "They're fin nippers."

"You can't do anything about that," Tucker said.

"I can *watch* it," Dinky said. "You should see all the torn fins. Torn fins all over the place."

On the way to the movie, Tucker told Natalia he thought Dinky was developing a cruel streak.

"You couldn't be more wrong," Natalia said. "The other afternoon this rummynose ate a hatchetfish, and Susan cried like a baby."

"There's still something freaky about the whole thing," Tucker said.

There were a lot of freaky things about that spring.

One was all the dope addicts pouring into DRI. Many of them were veterans the Army wasn't helping. Sometimes DRI couldn't even help them. The freaky thing about it was that they'd reenlist, because it was easier to get dope in the Army than out.

Even freakier was the fact they'd all sit around complaining how dope had wrecked them, and then they'd go back to it. They were the saddest losers Tucker had ever encountered.

It made Tucker think a lot about losing.

He spent so much time around Mrs. Hocker that he also began to think about this business of being a credit to the community.

To Tucker's mind, things had somehow gotten reversed. The community ought to be a credit to the person, and not the other way around.

It was the community that soldiers represented. If the community was all that right about war, the soldiers might feel less like losers.

Most of the members of DRI were blacks and Puerto Ricans, all from poor families. They were all losing in the community.

The community was a little like Mrs. Hocker: She meant well and everything, but she always seemed to be there *after* the damage was done. The best way to get Mrs. Hocker's attention was to get into some kind of trouble.

Tucker did a lot of thinking on a lot of subjects that spring.

There was this freaky thing about his relationship with Natalia, for instance.

His mother kept asking him if he and Natalia were going steady.

One conversation went like this:

"Have you asked her to go steady?"

"No."

"Well, that's very sensible. You're both too young to go steady."

"I'm not trying to be sensible, Mom."

"Then you don't want to go steady, is that it?"

"I don't see why we have to have an understanding about it."

"She might want to see other boys."

"I doubt it. She might."

"Would you mind that?"

"Maybe."

"You're all confused, aren't you?"

"No," he said. "I'm not confused at all."

He kept thinking, while he was talking with his mother, about this Beatle classic, "Something."

The words went, " 'You ask me if my love will grow. I don't know. I don't know.' "

That said it for him. It was the only possible answer, unless you could foretell the future.

But his mother said, "You shouldn't monopolize her time if you're not serious about her."

"I am serious about her."

"Have you told her that?"

"I guess she knows."

"I hope you're not too serious about her."

Sometimes he was so serious about her that he couldn't imagine his life without Natalia in it; other times he figured that someday in the far future, Natalia and he wouldn't even remember each other's names.

The physical part of their relationship was confusing, too.

Sometimes Tucker would daydream about her during his classes at Richter and miss an entire lecture. His body would actually feel her presence and remember the way she could affect him when they kissed or danced together, or stood on the Hockers' stoop saying good night. Other times he would be thinking of other things when they were together, even when their lips were pressed together; he would find himself thinking: *I ought to write P. John when I get home,* or *What am I going to write for that essay assignment, for Pete's sake?*

He didn't know if Natalia was going through the same thing or not.

What happened to Jingle that spring was also freaky.

Jingle got married again. His wife was this wiry little gray-haired Certified Public Accountant. She came to the town house one night in early April to help Tucker's father with his taxes. She brought along her own little adding machine, and she was able to sit there adding up long columns of numbers on it, at the same time carrying on a conversation and cracking jokes. Jingle kept making martinis for them, and talking about a vacation trip to Spain which they were going to take right after April 15th.

She called Jingle "Dollyface," and every time she laughed hard, she slapped her knee with her palm.

"Dollyface," she said, "tell them about the time that firm in Buffalo asked me to try and figure out why the workers were stealing sawdust."

"They were carrying sawdust out of the place every night by the wheelbarrowful," Jingle said. "Wheelbarrow after wheelbarrow of sawdust. The manager asked Evonne to figure out if they were selling the sawdust, or what the hell they were doing with it."

"That's right," Evonne said. "And you know what I found out? They were just dumping the sawdust. What they were stealing was wheelbarrows."

A freaky spring, all right.

Then suddenly it was May.

The first Friday in May, Tucker came home late from DRI one afternoon and found his father in the living room, talking with a stranger. He was a very tall, thin young man with rust-colored hair in a long, shaggy cut, and a pair of large steel-framed eyeglasses with blue-tinted lenses. He was in a faded blue workman's shirt, worn corduroy pants, and boots that laced. He was having a beer with Tucker's father.

"How've you been?" he said to Tucker.

Tucker put down his book bag, paused a moment, waiting for his father to introduce him, and then recognized him.

"P. John!"

P. John stayed for dinner, and right after dinner,

he called the Hockers. He asked to speak with Mrs. Hocker.

"I'd like to say hello to Susan," he said, "and I'd like to apologize for the way I behaved and thought last winter."

He was changed, all right, but in many ways he was the same old smooth, wiser-than-all-the-world P. John Knight.

Mrs. Hocker invited him over, and Tucker went along because he had a date that night with Natalia anyway.

Mrs. Hocker answered the door with her finger to her lips. "This is going to be a nice surprise for Dinky," she whispered. "Oh my my my my *my*— you have changed."

The thing was, Dinky had changed, too.

There are two ways of changing. One is to become more of what you once were, and one is to become less of what you once were.

P. John was less. He was less dictatorial and less unforgiving and unprejudiced, and his girth was less than it had ever been.

With Dinky, it was the other way around.

"There's a surprise out here for you, Dinky," Mrs. Hocker called out in her finest soprano.

"I'm *incapable* of being surprised," Dinky answered, while P. John grinned, as though to say, *That's Herself, all right,* "and I'm *trying* to get this tank back to a pH of 7!"

Natalia came down the hall and gave P. John a puzzled look, while Mrs. Hocker pressed her finger to her lips again. "It's P. John Knight," she whispered to Natalia. "Don't say anything."

Then Mrs. Hocker said, "Dinky, come out here this minute."

It took Dinky quite a bit longer than a minute. It would take anyone Dinky's size quite a bit longer than a minute to walk across her bedroom, down the hall, and into the foyer.

Since Tucker had only seen her in the half-light of the fish tanks every time he was at the Hockers', her size was a shock to him, too.

She was wearing a red kimono and a pair of old felt slippers which had once belonged to her father. Her face was bloated up like one of the blowfish Tucker had seen in her tank.

She blinked in the light, like a mole who lived in darkness. She said flatly, "Well, what's the big surprise," and then she turned the corner and saw P. John.

"Hello, Susan," P. John said.

She blinked some more, but she didn't twitch a muscle or let out a gasp or widen her eyes an inch.

"Hello, P. John," she said.

"How are you?"

"How do I look?"

"F-f-fine," he said. "Very good."

"I'm busy," she said, in that same flat tone.

Mrs. Hocker said, *"Dinky!"*

"I've got a pH below 7 in my tank," she said to P. John. "That's too acid, so you'll have to excuse me."

"I'd like to see your tank," he said.

174

She said, "In a pig's eye!" Then she turned around and started back down the hall.

"*Dinky!*" Mrs. Hocker said. "You come back here and apologize."

"It's not necessary," P. John said. "Please don't ask her to do that."

"I'm *very* ashamed of her," Mrs. Hocker said.

"Let her go," P. John said. "I don't think she needed a surprise like this."

The Heights Samaritan Banquet was held that Saturday night. P. John was invited, but he had to be back at Leeds to settle another labor dispute there. He didn't have much to say about Dinky after they left the Hockers' the night before the banquet; he didn't have much to say about anything, which surprised Tucker, because during dinner he had done practically all the talking.

The only comment he did make was an obscure one, about Dinky's new hobby. He said, "Fish die belly-upward, too."

The whole community showed up for the banquet; at least, it was Mrs. Hocker's version of "the community." Everyone to whom the name Helen Hocker was synonymous with Good Shepherd, Sydney Carton, or Mrs. Greatheart. Ministers, ladies' club presidents, local politicians, social counselors, psychologists, everyone from DRI, and all previous recipients of the Good Samaritan Award.

There were elaborate displays dealing with the problem of addiction: graphic illustrations of the jargon; actual needles, pills, and samples of heroin and cocaine encased in plastic; testimonies of former junkies, and charts depicting the relationship between addiction and the rise in crime.

Tucker sat with his mother and father, and held two seats for Natalia and Dinky.

Just before the program began, Natalia arrived alone.

"Susan's stuck back at the house," she whispered to Tucker as the Master of Ceremonies rapped for silence. "Something's wrong with the piston pump in the aquarium. She's going to come as soon as she can get it fixed."

There were many long speeches before the final one, which was the presentation of the award and the Samaritan statue.

It was one of those times Tucker was very turned on to Natalia, and she to him. They sat in the darkness of the crowded auditorium holding hands tightly.

The final speech was mainly about all the good work Mrs. Hocker had done rehabilitating dope addicts. During it, Mrs. Hocker had to wipe tears from her eyes a few times.

Then she made her speech, which was mercifully short:

"What pleases me most is that you're pleased with me. So long as I can serve my community well, I can hold my head high and give thanks to God that I found a way to be useful and responsible. Thank you."

Then, slowly, the community began filing out

of the banquet hall into the streets.

No matter what street you turned down, you saw it.

No matter how badly-lighted the street, it was large and visible and everywhere, in bright Day-Glo paint.

It was written on sidewalks, on curbstones, on walls, on the sides of buildings, and on the doors of automobiles.

It was every size and color.

DINKY HOCKER SHOOTS SMACK!

DINKY HOCKER SHOOTS SMACK!

DINKY HOCKER SHOOTS SMACK!

DINKY HOCKER SHOOTS SMACK!

DINKY HOCKER SHOOTS SMACK!

DINKY HOCKER SHOOTS SMACK!

It was there for the whole community to see.

SEVENTEEN

WHEN TUCKER and Natalia arrived back at the Hockers', they found Dinky, alone, in her bedroom, packing. There were paint stains all over her hands and face, and she was red-faced and breathless.

"I'm glad you're here," she said to Tucker. "I need someone to get my duffel bag down from the top of the closet."

"I thought something was wrong with the piston pump in your aquarium," Natalia said. "Was that all a big lie?"

Dinky slapped a pair of socks into an open suitcase on the bed. "I don't have time for explanations," she said. "In a matter of minutes the whole world's coming down on my head if I don't get out of here."

"You ought to wash up first," Tucker said.

"Your parents won't be here for a while," Natalia said. "Everyone's congratulating your mother."

"Stars don't stay stars for very long," Dinky said. "She might as well learn that." She glared at Tucker. "Are you going to get down my duffel bag, or let me break my back trying to get it down?"

"Why would you paint something like that all over the streets?" said Tucker. "Why would you do that to your mother tonight of all nights?"

"You're not shooting smack!" Natalia said.

"I'm not explaining my philosophy of life to you two, either," Dinky answered. "Where I'm going I won't owe anyone any explanations." She was dragging underwear from her bureau drawer to her bed, huffing and puffing with the effort.

"Sit down and collect yourself," Tucker said.

"Sit down and get caught red-handed by The Good Samaritan!" Dinky said sarcastically.

"Your hands are blue," Tucker said. "They're blue and green and gold."

Natalia said, "Wait a minute—wait. Listen. Susan, if you go in the bathroom and wash up, how will your mother know you were the one who painted all that over everything?"

"Because she has a way of ferreting out the truth —instantly!" said Dinky. "She has radar, second sight and a third eye!"

Tucker shook his head from side to side, biting away an irrepressible smile. "I'd just like to see the look on her face when she sees it," he said.

"Why didn't you stick around for a look at the look on her face?" Dinky said. "What good are you two? I want my duffel bag, Tucker!"

"I just *couldn't* stick around," Natalia said.

"I'll get your duffel bag down if you'll tell me where you're going," said Tucker.

"Don't try to blackmail me. I'll get it down myself," she said. "The reason you didn't stick around was because you thought you'd sneak in some time to make out before they come home."

"We came back here to find you," Natalia said.

"You knew I wouldn't be here!" Dinky said.

"You're here, aren't you?" Tucker said. "You're not a mirage, are you?"

"I'm practically gone." said Dinky. "You came back here to mouth a lot of mush to each other."

"Oh, Dinky," Natalia said, "why can't we reach you?"

"That's a good question," Dinky said. "It's certainly not because there isn't enough of me to reach."

She began to drag a chair over to the closet. She tried to stand on the chair, but was too exhausted, and just stood bent over it, holding the sides, catching her breath.

Tucker went across and put his hand on her shoulder. "Take it easy, Susan. I promise you that if your parents come in the front door, we'll lie and say we saw you heading into the deli. You'll have more time while they look for you."

"They probably haven't even left the banquet hall yet," Natalia said.

Dinky sat down on the chair. She fanned herself with her hand. After a few seconds, while she caught her breath, she said, "How was it going over with people?"

"Well, everyone noticed it," Tucker said. "You couldn't miss it."

"I made sure of that," Dinky said. "How did it go over?"

"People just kept repeating it: 'Dinky Hocker Shoots Smack, Dinky Hocker Shoots Smack,' " said Natalia. "I heard one woman say, 'That's Helen Hocker's little girl. They call her Dinky.' "

"I'm not unknown in Brooklyn Heights," Dinky said with considerable satisfaction.

"Where are you planning to go, anyway?" Tucker asked.

"Don't try to trip me up when my guard is down," Dinky answered. "Go on in the front room and make out. That's why you came here."

"No, it isn't," Natalia said.

"Yes it is!" Dinky said. "Maybe it wasn't at the time when I used to tease you that it was, but it is now. Everything's changed."

"Nothing's really changed," Tucker knelt down by the chair.

"Oh, get off your knees, jackass," Dinky said. "Everything has so changed, and about the lousiest thing I've ever had pulled on me in my entire life was pulled on me last night by you two *ex*-friends!"

"What?" Natalia said. "Tell us what."

"Tell you *what?*" Dinky hollered. "You don't know *what?* How could you let me waddle out in all my glory in front of that thinned-down storm trooper, who only came here to show off his weight loss in the first place?"

"He came here to see you," Tucker said, "not to show off."

"Bilgewater! And *you* dragged him over here!"

"He wanted to say hello," Natalia said.

"What if you'd gone crazier, instead of getting better?" Dinky asked her. "Would you like a surprise like that if you'd gone crazier? I got fatter since he saw me last, in case you didn't notice! And that was a nice fat surprise!"

Tucker and Natalia couldn't think of anything to say.

Dinky said, "Even that freaked-out street cat took a turn for the better. My mother told me that screwed-up alley cat has become a real tamebrain!"

Tucker said, "Susan?"

"My name is Dinky, El Creep-O!"

"Dinky," Tucker said, "we're really sorry about last night. We just didn't think, I guess."

"Now it's 'we,' is it? You're really joined at the hip," she said.

"You better go home, Tucker," Natalia said. "Would you mind?"

"I understand," said Tucker. "Sure."

"Oh, I love it, I love it, I love it," Dinky said. "They have this deep and meaningful relationship of mutual understanding."

"Good night, Susan," Tucker said softly.

"Susan," said Dinky, "has been swallowed up

and suffocated by the oily, solid substance in animal tissue; she has been strangled by suet."

"I'll call you tomorrow," Tucker said.

"Bug off, El Traitor."

Natalia walked him halfway down the hall.

"Are you sure you can handle this?" Tucker whispered.

"She's about to break down and bawl," Natalia answered. "I know her. She hates to have people see her cry."

"What if she really does run away?"

"Tucker, she's not going to *run* anywhere tonight. She's ready to collapse."

"If you need me—" Tucker said.

"I know," Natalia said.

"I feel like a louse."

"Lice," Natalia agreed.

On his way down Remsen Street, Tucker saw Mr. and Mrs. Hocker coming toward him. Tucker crossed the street. He darted into the shadows of the brownstones and began walking very fast.

"Tucker? Tucker Woolf?" It was Mr. Hocker's voice.

Tucker went even faster, without turning around once or looking over his shoulder. He was almost running when he heard the sound of footsteps running after him.

"TUCKER WOOLF!"

Tucker stopped then.

Mr. Hocker was alone. He came toward Tucker

with his necktie flying in the breeze, and Tucker noticed that his hands were balled into fists at his side.

"Just where were you going?" he said when he reached Tucker.

"Home."

"Where's Natalia?"

"Home. I just dropped her off."

"Is Dinky with her?"

Tucker remembered his promise to Dinky. He wasn't sure that it made any sense, with Mrs. Hocker already on her way there, but he didn't want to chance coming off as El Traitor a second time.

"I don't know," he said.

"Did you have a part in this, Tucker?" Mr. Hocker said.

"In what, Sir?"

"You know *what*, young man. Did you paint any of that around the streets?"

"No, Sir."

"I didn't think you did. But I'm not so sure, now, that you're not implicated in some way."

"I'm not implicated," Tucker said as though he were on trial in a courtroom.

"Then why did you try to avoid Mrs. Hocker and me just now?"

"I have to get home," Tucker said.

"Is Dinky with Natalia?"

Maybe Natalia was hiding Dinky, for all Tucker knew. She probably was. Dinky was in no condition to see her mother.

"Dinky might have gone to the deli," Tucker said.

"You're implicated, all right," Mr. Hocker said. "I know a guilty party when I talk to one."

"I'm not implicated. I'm just telling you where she might be, in case you and Mrs. Hocker want to go look for her."

"Mrs. Hocker isn't in any shape to go anywhere, and I think you can appreciate why she isn't."

"I'm really sorry, Sir," Tucker said.

Tucker felt sorry for Natalia, left back there to face Mrs. Hocker and to hide Dinky at the same time.

"You come along to the deli with me, Tucker," Mr. Hocker said.

Then Tucker felt sorry for himself.

They walked awhile wordlessly, and finally Mr. Hocker said, "This isn't just an average practical joke. I wonder if you appreciate that."

"I appreciate that."

"It has more serious implications."

Tucker was nervously aware of the way Mr. Hocker kept using the words "implicated," and "implications." He also wondered what would happen when they reached the deli.

Mr. Hocker said, "You might as well tell me the truth right now, because the whole truth is going to come out: did you and Natalia have any foreknowledge of this?"

"No, Sir."

"Why did you leave Natalia so early tonight?"

"I just did."

"And you haven't seen Dinky since the banquet?"

Tucker swallowed hard. "No, Sir."

"Then what makes you think she's at the deli?"

"A hunch."

"A *hunch*," Mr. Hocker said snidely.

Tucker didn't say anything.

"Do you know how deeply this has hurt Mrs. Hocker?" Mr. Hocker said.

"I suppose it would," said Tucker.

"I don't understand how Dinky could let a thing like this happen," Mr. Hocker said.

"What makes you think she's involved?" Tucker asked.

"A *hunch*," Mr. Hocker said snidely again. "Sometimes she can be very cruel."

"Last night," Tucker said, "we were pretty cruel to her. You weren't there."

"What do you mean?" Mr. Hocker said.

Tucker told him about bringing P. John over and surprising Dinky that way. He also reminded him of Christmas day when Mrs. Hocker made her little anti-P. John speech.

Mr. Hocker listened until Tucker was completely finished.

Then Mr. Hocker shrugged. "Well, Helen never really took the thing that seriously," he said, as though he were talking to himself.

"I think it was more than 'a thing' where Susan was concerned."

"It never amounted to much, after all," Mr. Hocker said.

"If it wasn't much," Tucker said, "it was still all Susan ever had."

They were walking down Hicks Street at that point. Mr. Hocker remained silent. They were minutes away from the deli. Tucker glanced at Mr. Hocker, who was frowning and walking with his head down.

Tucker finally cleared his throat and said, "She's home, Sir."

Mr. Hocker stopped walking and so did Tucker.

"What's all this *about*, Tucker?" Mr. Hocker asked.

Tucker's words came slowly. "I think it's about things amounting to a lot more than people think they amount to—I think it's about having your feelings shoved aside."

Mr. Hocker shook his head, "No, that isn't what I meant. I meant why did you tell me she's at the deli when she isn't?"

"*I* was talking about what *Susan* meant, for once," Tucker said. "People who don't shoot smack have problems, too."

Mr. Hocker looked at Tucker for a long moment. He looked away and gave the pavement a slight kick with his foot. Then he looked back at Tucker.

He said, "And Susan's safely home?"

Tucker nodded, and smiled slightly . . . not at Mr. Hocker, exactly; more at the soft sound, "Susan."

EIGHTEEN

"TUCKER," his mother said one early morning in late June, "did you finally finish setting up the library at DRI?"

"Not yet," he answered. "I'm waiting for fall."

They were driving across the Brooklyn Bridge. They were leaving for vacation, a camping trip to Bear Mountain; just the three of them, and Nader.

Tucker doubted that it was going to be much of a vacation for him. The back seat had a box full of pots and pans on it. Tucker's father had brought along a fishing pole to keep himself busy, and his mother had brought along one volume on federal estate and gift taxation, and another on suretyship.

"How is DRI doing without Mrs. Hocker?" Tucker's father asked.

"I guess some people miss her," Tucker said.

"I hope they're having a good time in Europe,"

his mother said. "Poor Helen will never live down that humiliation."

"She'll recover," Mr. Woolf said. "She's a very resilient woman."

"They're in Venice," Tucker said. "Natalia got a card from Susan with a picture of them riding in a gondola."

"Was it afloat, or slowly sinking into the canal?" his father chuckled.

"That isn't funny," Mrs. Woolf said. "The Hockers are doing everything to help her lose weight, and they're doing everything they can think of to show Susan how much they love her."

"I think I'll put on a little weight, and see if I can get a trip to Europe out of you two," Tucker said.

"If you can put on weight eating your own cooking, you'll deserve a trip to Europe," his father said.

"Tucker's getting to be a very good cook," his mother said, "and he never complains about it."

"You just never hear his bitching," Mr. Woolf said. "All the while he cooks, he mutters under his breath. Some day it'll all come out, I suppose, dramatically, Dinky Hocker style. Right, Son?"

"Right," Tucker said. "For the meek shall inherit the shaft."

"What'd you say, Tucker?" his mother asked.

"Nothing. Just something Susan said once about speaking out."

"She could write the book on *that* subject," Mr. Woolf said.

Tucker smiled. "P. John Knight used to say that inside every fat person, there's a thin person who wants to get out. Well, Susan got out from inside Dinky. Even Mrs. Hocker acknowledges that now; even she doesn't call her Dinky anymore."

They turned up the East River Drive, and Tucker sat in the back beside the box of pots and pans, petting Nader.

Nader had turned into this real together cat. It was Nader who was the connecting link—to life before Tucker had found her under the Chevrolet and life now. Only seven months had passed; it seemed like more.

For the summer, while Susan was off with her parents, Natalia was helping out at Renaissance. Tucker had a job in the Heights library, which would start when he returned from Bear Mountain.

He had already received two letters from Natalia, and he had written three to her. They probably wouldn't see each other until September. Both of them would be sixteen then.

At some point on their way up the Thomas E. Dewey Thruway, Tucker's mother said, "How do things stand between you and Natalia now?"

"Like the library at DRI," Tucker answered.

"Don't talk in riddles," his mother said. "What do you mean?"

Tucker said, "I'm waiting for fall."